Butterflies *in* My Bonnet

Sneak Peek into Life

PRANTIK MITRA

INDIA • SINGAPORE • MALAYSIA

ISBN 979-8-88555-979-9

Dedicated to My Late Father Dr. Nabakumar Mitra
And my Friends Anjan Bannerjee and Indrajit Dey who could not survive the Covid and left for their heavenly abode. I miss them all.

PREFACE FROM THE DAUGHTER

Stories are what makes people, as they're the only thing that stand out when memories fade away.

My father strongly embedded these words in his heart when he wrote this book.

He's always been of an inspiration to me. From his passion of books to movies, he's always had a knack of finding the marvels in reality. His way of narrating an incident has so much life, that sometimes it seems more real than your own experiences.

The pages of this book do justice to what his vision has always been. Since when I was young, I've always hoped that one day he compiles all his anecdotes into one treasure box.

The box is this book, and anyone who has the honour of reading it holds the key.

I can promise that this book is a revisit of your own memories, of jokes and anecdotes, of narrations woven into stories, of family, of friends and of thoughts, the juxtaposition of the old and new makes this a melting pot of joy.

A collection of short stories, most of them meant to make you laugh, cry and even think.

This book is like a warm cup of tea. Reminding you of home, with the little spark of imaginative reality, these stories will leave you with either a smile or a thought or both.

I think what truly sets this apart from any other anthology of books is the sheet relatability of it.

The most beautiful stories are woven out of our daily lives. The mishaps, the victories and the achievements. And when we find the corners to create everlasting art in that, is when we immortalize ourselves in the history of humanity.

These stories do that.

Reading this almost feels like your own life poetry, in the few pages of literary mastery that's been stitched into these stories.

Annayshi Mitra

Credentials: Daughter

Hello Readers,

Thanks for holding the book. The next step is to read it. Of course, you know that.

It is a choice though and I wish that you exercise the choice to read it.

There is an MCQ at the end which will test whether you have read it. So, read on even if you find it less interesting. Aha, got you there—Just Kidding.

This is my first attempt in bringing out a book of compilation of stories. All the more you should read it.

Most of the stories are either from real life or through fictionalization of local jokes into stories. Some have been taken from narrations by friends or Whatsapp forwards. I have taken the writer's privilege in doing so.

The pictures have largely come from the Internet. The intention has been to use freely usable pictures.

Trying to find a name to this effort was very difficult. I requested many to supply me with names for this book, but they never reverted. I don't blame them. They did not want to be forced to read a book named by them.

I remembered the phrase ***"Bee in my bonnet".*** This generally means that one is continuously and obsessively worried or disturbed about something. I literally thought that a bee buzzing away or threatening to sting inside your bonnet could be disturbing indeed. It was all about the bee I thought and not about the bonnet.

The foolish day dreamer that I am, I thought what if it was a butterfly instead of a bee. Everybody likes butterflies. They are beautiful, soft, charming, elegant and neither buzz like a bee nor sting like a bee. They fly effortlessly and gracefully and perch elegantly. They come in myriads of colors and make you feel happy.

This suggested to me that ***"Butterfly in my bonnet"*** would be a happy situation and everyone would want to have butterflies in their bonnet.

I also felt that this name could do some justice as the stories here are of various hues. I have, in my own way, defined the genre of the story. Maybe they represent the various colors of the butterflies and they do not buzz or sting.

I have many more stories in my head. A small joke that I hear, a small one min video that I see, something which I observe in real life all spring in my brain in the format of a story and then I start weaving around it and bring in characters and make them part of the story. I generally want to add a dash of humour to these.

Therefore, read these stories with a smile on your face else the story might make you smile and you might then think why did I not smile in the first place.

In absence of suggestions and in the lack of a proper method of naming the book I have settled for ***"Butterflies in my bonnet"***.

To each your own butterfly.

Two butterflies went out at noon

And waltzed above a stream,

Then stepped straight through the firmament

And rested on a beam

Lovingly Yours

Prantik Mitra

CONTENTS

S. No.	Story Title	Page Number
1	Happy at Work: Not Really	13
2	Breaking Free: A Clarion Call	24
3	But for the Indian Railways	49
4	Passing of a Soul Foretold – A Chronicle	54
5	Om Shanti Om	60
6	Harathi Nimeshaath Kaala Sarvam	72
7	Relationships have their Taste Too	77
8	Mother Oh Mother	88
9	Sacchu Da – The Officer	91
10	Inertia of Motion	99
11	Mistaken Identity	108
12	A Shattering Experience	113

13	Cart Before the Horse	122
14	It is My Kingdom, and I Am the King: Trilogy	135
15	Mouse Through the Drain	147
16	Now You See Me Now You Don't	157
17	Dronacharaya Cannot Lose	166
18	Swim, Wrap and Scoot	174
19	Dog Chain	183
20	MOU-Conditions Apply	194
21	Happy Birthday – Oops	201
22	Coronation	208

HAPPY AT WORK: NOT REALLY

Genre: Philosophy, Well sort of

Doing a job is necessary.

You need to earn your bread and perhaps your butter too.

For some it's just an arduous trek out of sheer necessity, for many it's a monotonous humdrum routine. There are a very few who really enjoy it and even fewer who go to sleep with the ecstatic feeling of going back to the office yet again, come tomorrow.

So, what's the deterrent……???

The Boss, the nature of work, which is not to the liking of the employee, the fear of failure, the environment, the inability to speak out, the office politics, lack of democracy and transparency and what not. In the world stage of today there are more job seekers than jobs available so there is a chase for something in which one could lose out or settle for something lower and maybe meaner than what one was aiming for.

Therefore, you start with a compromise and more often than not live with the compromise for your entire career.

The aim dies a natural death and often visions of what would have been had you been so and so and so and so keep haunting.

Once you have been forced to settle with the plain vanilla your want for the other exotic flavors dies and the routine of the plain vanilla takes up your time.

So, what does one do?

Well good question the answer to which has been elusive. Some have broken free to chase their dreams while most have reconciled to the quicksand of forbidden dreams.

But then like the wary desert traveler with the camel as his companion one must look for an oasis and with some perseverance, patience, strong resolution and never give up Mantra one can find it. The Oasis brings in the much-needed relief and a vision which could still look bizarre and improbable but not impossible.

Impossible is nothing they say.

Where is this oasis at the workplace?

How do you find this Oasis?

How can you pursue the effort to finding this Oasis?

What do you expect this Oasis to be?

Once you find it what next?

Hold on. We will talk about this later while all those who happen to read this can make this interactive for me by telling what their perception of this Oasis is. Better still it would be nice to locate someone who has found this Oasis. What did it mean to him? What did it lead to?

Look this is not about breaking free and the dance of the dragons. It is about bringing back the dream bit by bit into the desert where you thought you had lost your way.

Long Long ago —well not so long ago i.e., in 1995, 1996 I would travel to office in a chartered bus. Let me tell you all about what a Chartered bus is about in the city of Kolkata in India. Here various office goers more or less in the same route get together and hire a bus for commuting to and from the office and run it on their own usually without any profit.

Therefore, the bus is hired more or less on a wet lease along with the driver and helper at a monthly rental and then a pool of office goers is created. These office goers are given membership passes on an annual or monthly basis and they can then avail this bus to commute to and from office and the bus plies on a specified route. These chartered buses are fun as the bunch of people from diverse organizations get together, get to know each other, become friendly and so on. This group usually also has its own outings, picnics and so on.

However, this is not about the concept of the Chartered bus but about the workplace, the pains, travails and joys and the oasis.

On my way back from office I would usually sit on one of the front seats just behind the front door. At the door would stand a youngish looking lad maybe in his late twenties and he was the helper of the bus. The job of such helpers is to announce the route of the bus, help people get in and usher them in, announce the next stop, give directions to the driver as to slow down or stop if a passenger so desired. A very tedious and difficult job for all practical purposes and specially during the hot and humid days of summer when the relative humidity would be as close to 99% and the temperatures touching or even crossing 40 deg C.

Owing to my seating position at the bus I would keep chatting a bit with this boy. He came from a poor family, was a graduate and was on the lookout for a better job. However, I observed that he had a very lively attitude, a 24X7 smile, cheerful demeanor and everyone in the bus liked him. Many a times when the bus would ply at full speed, he would just hold the handle, stand at the door and sing some song or other in not too bad a voice. Over a period of time, he knew everyone of us by name and also knew the stop at which we would get down and he would call us quite in advance by name before the stop came. He would ask us about our family and wellbeing and if you happened to be absent on a particular day, he would remember to check on you if everything was okay. He was the live wire of the bus. Many of our fellow office goers who would leave the bus due to change of jobs and thereby a change of route would miss him and once a while take a detour to catch this bus of ours just to meet him.

We couldn't do much for this boy except giving him small gifts and sweets on occasions, invite him to our bus member picnics and he would always be the live wire with the added caution of not crossing his limits at any point of time.

The fact that I can recall him and talk and write about him even after twenty years is a case in point. I am not in touch with him and do not have his whereabouts but the thought of taking the bus, watching his liveliness, hear him sing still brings a smile to my lips. He affected my life in a positive way. Why? How?

....

I had asked him once what he enjoyed about such a tough job and he said " Sir the fact that I know you by name, announce your stop while similarly I know all in the bus and know their stops and the fact that all of you feel so relaxed with the thought that I am there to announce your stop well in advance and the faith you have in me is a great blessing which I a am sure will keep bringing happiness in my life". He further moved on to say "In my bad days even if five of you pray to God for me I am sure one of your prayers will get answered and that is such a great feeling". So, I asked him what got him going the job or we the members of the bus. He said, "Sir but for the bus how would I know its members"?

This second line has been a lingering thought in my mind.

What was it about this boy's job that kept him happy? The job itself or the other things and the other people that came to him because of the job.

The cause of the because as one of my friends says.

His job was to announce stops, usher in and help bus members and if you were to write his JD what would you write?? The fact that he interacted with all of us in a positive way without fear or favor and we responded back was not part of his JD. So, did he exceed his brief? Is it okay to transgress your brief and if yes how and when?

Therefore, does the oasis lie not in the job but in the other things that it brings with it? Are we all able to identify these other things?

I have a friend and engineer who got recruited from the campus and got placed with a good Corporate in India in the textile industry. Textile Industry had been his academics and he was happy to get the job.

He carried great illusions about the job as most engineering graduates do only to realize that what you learn and eventually what you do are extremely different. Moreover, his work was largely clerical, scrutinizing papers and bills and invoices and so on and the job also meant sitting for late hours in office.

He carried on with detest and loathing for the job and often wondered what to do. He was looking for his Oasis.

While he would return home at night and traverse the road to home through the public transport in the city of Kolkata he would look out of the window of the moving bus and tram and observe the people on the roads and pavements of the city. He found life in them.

At Kolkata like many other cities of India several people live on and along the pavements and eat and cook there too. They are largely poor, labor class people and workers.

My friend recalls that on his way home he would even watch these people sitting along the roadside on pavements and signing together and cooking food on their makeshift *chullas (This is an Indian earthen oven fired by coal and/or wood and used for cooking).*

And looking at this he would often wonder than even these people who were poor, lived hand to mouth, dwelled in pavements, did arduous and bone breaking labour job during the day had the gumption and liveliness to gather together, sing together and cook their food. He felt their happiness and was envious.

It was joy and envy combined that started creating a fire within him.

He watched them every day and he actually reached a stage of life where he would wait for office to end so that on his way back home, he could watch and savour the life and delight of these people. They attracted him, they made him happy.

He felt even these people had everyday moments when they would forget everything and just be happy.

The Question is was this his trigger in search of an Oasis—within or without?????

One day this friend of mine came to my office and proudly announced that he had resigned from his job and was happy and free. As to whether he had got another job he said NO. As to his plans for the future he was blank. I was stunned. He had a large family to carry, his father had retired, and his sisters were still studying, and I knew jobs in India were not abundant enough for your picking. Together we went to another friend, and we counseled him, but he was adamant.

He was having no more of that drudgery… He had snapped…and made his decision.

Gradually he picked up his beans and started his own business of trading in textiles and to cut a long story short he is successful, happy and contented now and freely advises us to give up our jobs.

"Once determined the rest is easy", he says…

He did find his Oasis but outside his job… There was a trigger to do so… But all of us have so many triggers but keep compromising and compromising…

Well, why do we need the Oasis at all:

- We are in a job out of necessity and the job is not to our liking?
- Not able to meet the expectations of the boss?
- The remuneration (financial) is not enough?
- Many other people are being given greater importance.
- Unhappiness at the personal/domestic front leading to lack of concentration at office?
- Very stiff targets?
- Setting for oneself a mission and not being able to accomplish it?
- Poor and shoddy office environment?
- Distractions in office?
- Threats from outsiders?
- Threats from insiders?
- Very little personal and social time?
- Long commuting distance to and fro?
- Fear of failure?
- Too organized and idealistic?
- Improper processes, poor controls, indiscipline?

- Physical and health challenges?
- Not able to manage subordinates?
- Run of the mill activity?
- Perception of peers?
- Routine, clerical activity with no challenge thrown in?
- Very late hours?
- Shift duty thereby disrupting biological rhythm of the body.
- Mismatch with expectations?
- Lack of recognition?
- Promotional issues?
- Locational problems?
- Unhealthy conditions?
- Peer Pressure

Have I missed any?

What's the choice for a job? Money or Nature of Job? Which carries greater weightage?

Can the two be balanced?

WHAT DO WE ACTUALLY WANT FROM A JOB?

To leave something, especially when you need to drop steady finances, and to plunge into a passion is not easy but there are enough examples of people having done it. You can search them out there are plenty.

What have they all in common? They just held on to their passion failure after failure.

Check out the life story of Jack Ma…

Check out the story of Marvan Attapatu Srilankan Cricketer.

Take a plunge that's the mantra. At least you won't regret having not tried.

BREAKING FREE: A CLARION CALL

Genre: Crazy Travelogue of college and hostel days. Do not try it except under parental guidance

The day began as usual. Well in hostels that too in Engineering College Hostels the mornings are generally lazy as students try and force themselves out of their slumber, nurse a hangover, look lost and / or go back to sleep again. Breakfast generally runs cold and many a times the morning tea is usually followed soon with lunch. Many a times even before a shave or a bath and sometimes even before the morning rituals. Did someone say, "What about college and classes"? Frankly who cared.

It was the month of March and *Holi* Holidays (Indian Festival of Colors) had just gone by. The students were spiritually enlightened (literally) and the festive mood was lingering on. There was a football game in the evening where Vivek defended well, so did Utpal, Jhilik as usual dribbled the ball well, Prantik was the striker, Saibal was at the hostel doing his routine exercises, Dhruva was also at the hostel sitting on the broken bed supported at the end of the long corridor of the hostel, Alok had gone out to the city and Snehangshu was happily puffing on to his Wills Navy Cut Cigarette and chatting with Dhruva.

The football game ended around 6 PM and after light showers and wash the gang collected on the broken wooden bed. This was chit chat time, passing around of cigarettes, a bit of weed, jokes and unblemished pure fun.

Normally energy in such hostel's peaks after dinner and a game of Bridge was suggested by Snehangshu which religiously began at around 1130 in the night. Almost the entire 3 rd year batch was there. Four playing, the others watching and the balance lazing around smoking, commenting, cheering. As the night grew old and the card game of bridge became a bit heavy for the mind it got replaced by flush- Teen Patti (The three-card game). Three Card Brag is a gambling game played with a standard 52 card pack without jokers. The cards in each suit rank in the usual order from high to low: A-K-Q-J.

Teen-Patti (three card game)started sometime at 2.30 AM in the night and more people joined in. In came Roopak, Pranab, Sridip etc. Board money was kept light and seen had to stake double of the blind. So ran the game cutting the darkness of the night amidst bits and pieces of fights, debates, skirmishes and the jingling of the coins at play. There were obviously pee breaks.

At one such collective pee break Vivek pointed out that it was about 5.30 AM in the morning and the radiance of the dawn was filtering in.

Phew...... whole night at cards and a wonderful dawn. Sridip gave a clarion call to walk down to the bus stop for tea and some *Sar Rooti* (Bread laced with milk cream, sprinkled with sugar, turned upside down with the cream laced side facing downwards and toasted over coal fire).

The gang then dressed up and left. Some went to sleep but Vivek, Alok, Dhruva, Sridip, Utpal, Prantik, Saibal, Jhilik, Snehangshu sauntered down to the bus stop. Tea, Toast and some smoking followed when someone in the team set the tone for adventure suggesting that we hail a truck and hitch hike a ride to the Farakkah Dam from the Behrampore bus stop. 3rd year Engineering students in their early twenties had got their trigger and the resolution was unanimously passed. A quick counting of money was made and INR 220 (In the year 1986) was counted on deck as everyone dumped their money into a common pool. Not much but not too bad and then the *hail-a-truck* process was set in motion.

Flagging down a truck for students was not too uphill a task and soon Alok and Sridip were haggling with a truck driver on the rate for the hike. Four climbed on to the cabin and five at the back as the deal was settled for INR 60.

The journey was fun specially for the five at the back as they dumped themselves on the sacks of cargo being carried and Snehangshu lit a cigarette which was gleefully passed around. The journey was lovely through the countryside and Saibal broke into a song to be hooted down by others. Prantik dozed off and so did a few others to be nudged back to reality by Vivek who miraculously had produced a pocket-knife from nowhere and had cut upon the sacks to reveal a cargo of *gur* (Jaggery).

Quickly four / five pellets were pulled out for pilfering and another pellet was eaten on the spot. For empty hungry stomachs this was manna from heaven. The journey thus took a sweet turn with the balance of the gang in the cabin completely oblivious to this unethical pilferage. Cigarette and bites of gur (jaggery) seemed to go quite well together. After about three hours, it was nearing 930AM Farakkah was announced, and the gang jumped out of the truck. The place looked amazing, and the Farakkah Barrage looked gorgeous and mammoth. Most of the barrage gates were closed and the river fully contained on one side only seemed to trickle out into a narrow stream at the other side. After some time, a nice sitting place just beside the river was located as everybody sat down to relax and smoke. Cigarettes were also filled with weed (ganja) and passed around. The river breeze, the stillness of the place, the sparkle of the sun on the river, the giant of a dam made for a perfect setting for these adventure and ganja (not all had) laden youths. The icing on the cake was the availability of pilfered gur (jaggery) which served as brunch and kept hunger at bay.

Three hours went buy when Alok announced that we could further hitch hike to Malda. Unanimity of this sudden idea took time with Snehangshu dropping out to head back to hostel. Neither coaxing nor the choicest of slangs could get him to agree. The others took it forward as again the process of hailing another truck was set in motion…

At this point let me introduce the gang in short sentences where I shall try to capture the individual quintessence.

Jhilik Biswas: Medium height and stocky. Very jovial and jolly and an excellent footballer. He was a master at dribbling and passing the ball.

Vivek Agarwal: Hailed from Delhi. Fair, tall and handsome. Easily blended into the West Bengal Culture and in two years was speaking fluent bengali and by the third year could even read Bengali. Cool, composed and tension free.

Saibal Chakraborty: The body builder. Tall, fair and well built. Was rigorous and meticulous with his exercise regimen. Used to have two raw egg yolks every morning with milk. This allowed us to queue up in front of his room to collect (on first come basis) the white of the egg which would then be made into an egg white omelet.

Dhruva Pratim Ghatak: The eternal freak with almost a photographic memory and tremendous dare devilry. Absolute carefree soul who lived his life on his terms.

Alok: Quiet and highly under rated who popped out as the prize discovery on various occasions. A great artist and designer, he single-handedly conceptualized the design and layout of the Saraswati pandal and later (with manual help from others) also went ahead to create the structure of the pandal.

Utpal Maity: Excellent defender (football) who could also bring up surprise attacks. Named MARA (meaning dead) due to his lethargic attitude albeit could spring to life in a football game. Lively and jolly by nature.

Sridip: A bengali born and brought up in Assam made a heady combination. Source of our Assameese slangs, a great cricket batsman who went up to play at the district level but soon gave it away, a good footballer too. Highly energetic and lively. Could slice through the tensest of atmosphere through his jokes and wit.

Snehangshu: Loved his white Kurta Payjama (Indian Traditional dress), his wills navy cut cigarette and his bridge (card game). Spoke less but could join in the fun whenever required.

Prantik: Yours Truly

Two were selected to get down to flagging a truck.

We had close to INR 160 with us so the strategy this time was different. There was to be no discussion with the truck driver and helper, as soon as a truck would stop the idea was to just climb onto the back without seeking permission. Change in strategy required change in roles too. Readers can scroll back and read about the description of the individuals and guess which two were chosen for flagging down a truck.

Orders were simple and brief. These two would flag down the truck. Once the truck slowed down the others would scamper towards the back of the truck and haul themselves in while these two would engage the driver for 45 secs. Once the gang at the back was in, they would refuse to get down so that these two would then clamber on to the cabin. Money dealings for the ride would come later.

The plan was executed to perfection. Dhruva and Sridip (Flagged down the truck. Did anyone guess it right). In the process Dhruva removing his shirt and tying it around his waist. Vivek and Jhilik were the first to clamber on to the back hauling themselves quickly up by using the lock chains of the truck. The others followed suit and Snehangshu had to be pulled in. Dhruva and Sridip then climbed onto the cabin and were left to deal with the driver on price points. We later learnt that the driver had demanded INR 150 and Sridip and Dhruva had to use all their skills to get that scaled down to INR 30, of course this also involved exchange of the choicest expletives and threats to push the gang out of the truck midway but Sridip and Dhruva stood the test and en-route even managed to share a few *beedis* (an Indian version of a mini cigar filled with tobacco flakes, wrapped in tobacco leaf and tied with a string at one end) with the driver and his attendant.

Farakkah to Malda is around 34 Kms and the truck journey took about one hour.

It was post lunch time and the gang was tired and drowsy. The effects of gur and ganja were catching up and sleep beckoned. The back of the truck was empty and there was no cargo to pilfer. Everybody dozed off in fits and bursts. Jhilik however had kept awake holding onto the truck's rails, enjoying the countryside he had broken out to singing along the way. A heavy medley of Hindi, Bengali and Folk songs. Everyone was too tired to boo him down and he seemed too tired to stop.

Malda was announced and all climbed down with lazy steps. Everyone was hungry but money was scanty. A small budget was allotted for tea and snacks. Hot tea and a vegetable cutlet each while sitting on the bench of a local tea stall brought huge relief. A quick count of balance money was made. INR 100 and dwindling.

A bit rejuvenated everyone decided to stroll down to a garden and spend some time there. Cigarettes were still available. As evening drew near the group moved to the railway station with no definite plan. Once at the railway station there were debates on what to do next. Most suggested enough was enough and we should all return to the hostel. While this was still on the anvil the bomb dropped. Difficult to recall who dropped it but it did not burst but got defused by the spirit of further adventure. Probably Vivek and Saibal dropped the bomb by suggesting that a TTE (Traveler's Ticket Examiner in a Train) could be managed, and we could take a train to Siliguri. The idea was lapped up but money for dinner and further movement was not enough. Never to give up on adventure Sridip suddenly recalled that he had a maternal uncle at Malda working with the railways and if he could be located dinner and onward travel could get managed.

Note: Remember in those days there was no mobile phone and no internet.

Hip Hip Hurray... What a piece of news. The treasure hunt began...........

Locating the whereabouts of a Railway Man in the premises of the Indian Railways as it seemed in hindsight was quite an easy job. But hindsight is a matter of the future, and we were in the present. Dwindling money, tiredness and fatigue were showing up in bits and pieces though the sense of adventure kept suppressing them. Our attire too had become shabby and dirty and disheveled hairs added to the poignancy of the scene, if I may say so.

We huddled up and decided to break into groups of two to locate the gentleman. It was decided that we would quiz every railway man available at the station regarding this mysterious gentleman whose name we knew. Those, as I have said earlier too, were not the days of mobile phones so we decided to meet back at a particular tea stall after half an hour. Having planned thus "Operation Search" was flagged off.

Half an hour later each one came back to the meeting point to discover that Sridip and Dhruva had come back to the assembly point within ten minutes having located the whereabouts of this mysterious gentleman Mama. As we realized later Sridip and Dhruva had straight gone to the Station Masters' room to enquire about the gentleman and as it transpired the Station Master knew the Mama well and even provided us with the address of the house where he lived. On that particular day he was on night duty and was likely to be at home at this point of time. That was amazing news. The smile that started from Alok's lips completed the full circle through everybody's' lips ending up with a big hurray at the end.

Dhruva and Sridip scampered off to locate the Mama and his house while we spent our time gossiping at the station and observing the myriads of activities at the station. We even gathered up courage to spend money for a small cup of refreshing tea each. Very soon Sridip and Dhruva came back running brimming from Head to Toe. The Mama was located, and he had graciously invited us all for dinner. There was a silence of disbelief before we realized how hungry we all were and some home cooked dinner free of cost would just be the right thing to keep us going. Dinner was good though not lavish, hospitality was even better, and the best part was the Mama knew a TTE who could get us into the night train, onward bound to Siliguri, with a nominal amount of payment to him. The resolution was passed unanimously and after a wonderful dinner we trudged along with Mama back to the station.

There was a train coming in at around 11.00 in the night and Mama's friend would let us in the reserved compartment for a nominal fee of INR 60 and would also get us out of the Siliguri station at the Siliguri check point. The deal was done, and we waited for the train after sentimental goodbyes and thanks to Mama for his hospitality. We felt even more grateful to him when before leaving he handed over a INR 100 note to Sridip telling him to keep it for emergency. What he did not know was that we were already in emergency. Everybody would have hugged him but everybody in his own mind, as came out from discussions later, refrained lest it expose our true situation and our almost empty pockets.

The train chugged in, and we were ushered into a reserved compartment. The train was going up to Guwahati and there were lots of Assamese people in there which made our task easy as Sridip having been born and brought up in Assam knew the language and made friends easily to the extent that quite a few of them agreed to share their berths with us. What else would we have wanted, A healthy dinner, a 100 rupee note, a train to siliguri and to top it all few shared berths which could allow you at least half a sleep for the overnight journey.

Alok settled onto a berth and so did Sridip. It appeared as if it was Sridip's authorized berth and the legal reserved owner of the berth was actually being adjusted by Sridip. Saibal had found a sitting position. Utpal, Jhilik and Dhruva had spread themselves on the floor near the bathroom oblivious of the stench if any. Dhruva having used his old technique of opening his shirt and wearing it inside out (the logic was that when he would alight, he would wear it the right way again and only the inside part would be soiled and dirty).

Vivek and I opened the door of the train and sat there. The train started pulling out of the station through a shifting panorama of lights, vendors, tea stall, people waiting for their trains, coolies, hawkers of various kinds. They all started becoming a blur as it gathered speed and suddenly plunged into the darkness of the night leaving the station behind. Gusts of wind hit us as the train pierced into the silence of the night along with the rhythmic sound of the wheels on the tracks and the intermittent hooting of horn by the driver breaking the eerie silence of the night. The train was passing through vast expanses of agricultural land and the silhouette of trees in the darkness would almost appear ghostly.

I went into a reverie thinking of my parents at home and wondering if they have had their dinner by now, I thought of them missing me and felt sad, I thought of my mother and of home cooked food, I thought they would be thinking of me studying hard and felt guilty, I thought of the college hostel and wondered what the other students would be thinking about us, I thought of our hostel warden and felt that perhaps I was letting him down running away on adventure without information or notice. I had visions of my childhood. I was perhaps dozing of intermittently.

The sudden hooting of the horn shook me up from my reverie. I could see lights in the distance perhaps an approaching station. Dhruva had woken up and joined me and so did Utpal as the train pulled into a station. It was around 3.00 PM at night.

We alighted and took a stroll. Utpal lit a cigarette and we shared.

When we got back into the train again, I was very sleepy. I spread out on the floor and slept and dreamt of our new destination … Siliguri…

I was awakened by a beam of sunlight. I blinked, rubbed my eyes, found myself on the floor of what looked like a train. Few more seconds of eye rubbing, and reality sunk in. The train was moving on, the speed was slower. I got up and nudged the others awake. We were into the second day now.

We went to the door and peered out. Various railway lines were converging and diverging, the countryside had given away to an urban landscape, the train was slowing down, and it was imminent that a station was approaching. By now everyone of the gang was awake. We all felt and obviously looked shabby, dirty and unkempt.

Slowly the train entered the station and we finally alighted at Siliguri and were ushered out, without a problem. Once outside the station we were clueless where to head to when Jhilik suggested that we go to the Siliguri Tourism office as it opened early and also had a biggish reception for seating people as well as clean washrooms which could help with our morning chores. At the tourism office we took turns to wash up a bit and freshen up while someone from the gang kept the officials engaged with queries on sightseeing and tourism opportunities. Utpal was the last and when he announced bowels cleared, we were ready to move out of the office.

Our stomachs were cleared so to say and Jhilik had even had a shower using his shirt as the towel. There was no tooth paste on us, so we had to contend ourselves with a bit of rinsing the mouth with water and save Jhilik we were all without a bath and shave. However, shaving was not something that mattered to Dhruva as he was sporting a beard.

Thus, slightly freshened up and taking count of money which stood at INR 120/- we decided to walk down towards the bus and taxi stand. The bus and taxi stand were crowded with regular commuters and passengers. Being slightly early into the tourist season tourists had not yet started arriving. We spotted a minibus half occupied with the driver and helper calling out for people for Kalimpong. Before others could even realize Sridip, Alok and Saibal had started negotiating with the driver for a trip to Kalimpong.

The regular fare was around INR 30/- per head but the trio bargained for all of us for INR 30/- coaxing and cajoling and taking advantage of the fact that this was off season and that we were students, and the bus was not filling up in any case and that God would really bless the driver for helping students and so on and so forth.

However, at this point in time Jhilik panicked. He wanted to go back and urged us all to do so. How will you guys return with hardly any money left? He bellowed. He was booed down collectively, called a coward and Alok and Vivek gave him a good lecture on how one should live in the present and not think of the future. Jhilik was in no mood for sermon and returned it with the choicest expletives and got back more in return. The driver caught in the crossfire of this verbal duel quickly planted himself on his driver's seat and started honking madly and we thought he would drive away and so jumped in with Sridip throwing his final volley of abuses as he hung out of the bus at its footboard. Jhilik had already started walking away from the bus and the bus had started off too.

We settled down and started enjoying the journey. The bus crossed the Teesta Bridge and soon began its journey upwards through the winding mountain road. The hills emerged in their splendor, the winding road looked magical, the weather gradually started getting cooler and cooler, the long trees looked gorgeous, and the cliffs, gorges and occasional mountain streams made our hearts rejoice

The bus was largely filled with locals who got a bit friendly with us. One of them passed around a few apples which we devoured instantly as it brought some relief to our hungry stomachs.

The bus reached Kalimpong sometime late afternoon. We alighted to be greeted by a bit of cold weather, floating clouds, lush green hills and our hearts soared in excitement. Hunger had to be satisfied first and a small tea stall made our day by providing us with bread and tea at a very cheap rate. Hunger satisfied it was but felt apt that we should make the trip worthwhile by trying out a bit of sightseeing. Shivering in the cold but warm in the heart we approached a tourist jeep and the driver agreed to take us around Kalimpong at INR 30/- and cover the seven points. It was fun and the driver even shared a small bottle of rum with us which kept the cold at bay.

We enjoyed the sightseeing and followed it up with a group photo shoot (the studio owner agreed to send the photographs to us by VPP wherein we could pay on receipt of the photographs at the stated address).

It was getting dark, and we decided to return back to Siliguri. Stock taking showed up a meagre balance of INR 30/-. Enquiries at the bus stand revealed that the last bus had left. We were stranded and worried now. No money, no food and no place to stay at a hill station which was getting colder and colder as the night drew in. Desperate and frantic efforts and enquiries revealed that one local bus driver could manage for us shelter at a school for the night and we could then take the early morning bus. We had resigned to the fate when suddenly there emerged from the crowd (our predicament had drawn in many onlookers and sympathizers and being a very lean tourist season everyone had a lot of time to spend on us) a jeep driver stating that there is a bus which comes in at around 11 PM from a place called Rangli (dont know if I remember the name right now) provided the weather is good.

That was a chance we had to take, and we planted ourselves in a tea stall waiting with bated breath for the bus to arrive. Arrive it did sometime around midnight, and we jumped in. We got seats towards the last row and settled down only to realize that the bus had its rear windshield broken and cold air was floating in. We collapsed one over the other in our seats exhausted and shivering and one by one fell asleep………

At least… so, to say we were homeward bound……

Slumber makes good bedfellows with tired minds and tired bodies. Minor irritants like the twists and turns of a hilly road, blasts of cool breeze, the jerks and jolts of an otherwise creaky bus et al get ignored. However, the circadian rhythm of hunger pangs create a threshold, a point beyond which slumber fails and hunger takes over and the other irritants, so encouraged, sneak in too.

That surely must have been the case with me as I opened my eyes and looked around to find the others awake too. Too weary for conversation of any sort I looked around. The bus had descended from the mountains on to the plains, the breeze had a lesser bite, the dawn had painted the horizon with a lovely orangish hue and above all we had never discussed where to alight. Too tired to bring up the discussion I decided to stay on mute mode and perhaps carry on till the bus reached its final destination.

Caught between an aching body, a blank mind and a hungry stomach I was numb and had just allowed fatigue to take over when I heard Saibal and Alok urging us to shake ourselves up and prepare to get down. As if triggered into a chain reaction every one of us was on our feet and we had soon alighted the bus with Vivek and Saibal thanking the driver profusely for his generosity. Beyond us and across the road where we had alighted there was quite an open ground and a temple with an upraised platform. We all decided to go to the temple. The temple complex was nice and clean and the temple itself was on a large, elevated marble basement. The place was nice and clean, and we all settled down there. The marble floor was comfortable and there was a tube well nearby which helped us wash and clean ourselves a bit and also provided us with much needed drinking water.

A banana tree within the temple complex was sighted blooming with almost ripe bananas and was attacked immediately. Cool drinking water, and about one and a half banana each brought great respite and thus undisturbed and unperturbed in this serene surrounding and at a holy and religious place we one by one collapsed on the marble floor and fell asleep again.

When I woke up I found Sridip, Dhruva, Alok and Saibal missing. I learnt that Sridip had been able to remember the name and para (a particular location generally in a residential area) of a relative and along with Dhruva in tow had ventured out to trace him. Alok along with Saibal had gone out with fervor and hope to *no-one-knew* where.

The remaining of us could only wait with Vivek suggesting that we could try and do some manual labor ((carrying bricks: as in the distance a building construction was going on and daily laborer's had lined up looking for days work and the contractor was recruiting them one by one for the day after fixing up the *dihadi* (a term used for the rate for the day)) by lining up for work like the daily wagers and earn some money to see us through.

We even walked up to the Contractor only to scurry back without the gumption of trying to attempt the ask though in the bargain I could manage a few beedis from one of the labors and gleefully lit one and spread out again on the marble floor of the temple. We had our fits and bouts of conversation interspersed with dozing off when at around 12 Noon we spotted Dhruva and Sridip running towards the temple excited and brimming from ear to ear. They had brought great news. They had located the relative, fed them a cock and bull story of how we had come here to participate in a volleyball tournament, had got mugged and robbed on the way and were in desperate condition. The relative had wanted to come along for help, was cajoled not to and eventually in the end parting with INR 200 to help our cause of going back to the hostel.

Sridip and Dhruva had got some breakfast there too and had also brought few apples for us.

This was great news. We almost had our capital back and also some food, so the celebration was impromptu only to be interrupted by Alok and Saibal who had just come in to announce that lunch was organized, and we needed to quickly follow them and follow their instructions to the T.

In hindsight I feel that our silent prayers at the temple might have done it, till date I have not been able to find any other valid explanation except that there was a divine intervention.

On the way to our luncheon destination, we heard the story. Alok generally frequented a "MATHA" (A monastic order of Hindus. There are various MATHAS in India. A parallel can be drawn to Buddhist monasteries maybe) at his native place.

A brainwave sent him on the lookout for a similar" MATH" / a branch/ an affiliate etc and he ended up finding one. Reference to certain monks and names at his native place established his credentials and his story about our having run out of money while coming to participate in a tournament evoked sympathy and thereby an invitation for lunch.

As we reached the" MATH" we were greeted with warmth. The Head Monk himself came out to welcome us and Alok fell on a "Sashtang Dandavat" (A form of prostration wherein the devotee lies fully prostrate at the feet of an idol or spiritual leader with arms outstretched towards the idol/leader/guru) and we followed suit in awkward fashion. It would have looked like quite a comedy sequence to onlookers with seven people suddenly collapsing to the ground in unison.

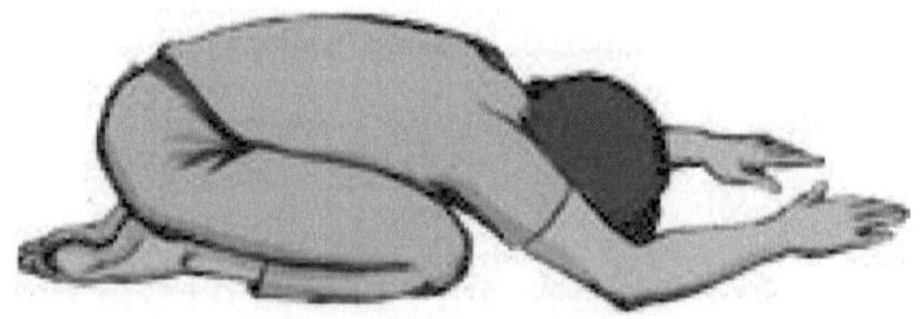

We were blessed profusely by the monks, sympathized on our predicament and led to lunch after washing our hand and feet. We sat down on the floor with other monks for the lunch.

Till date I cannot forget the meal. It was like sharing a meal with GOD. The food was simple and extremely tasty. The meal was filling replete with warm milk, hot steamed rice, two extremely tasty curries, lentil and salads, some pickles and chutney (an Indian sauce made in various ways), papad (crisp, generally disc shaped food made from seasoned dough usually of gram flour) and lots and lots of love. We were famished and this was heaven. The conversation with monks was kept by Alok. In any case we were under strict instructions from him to speak less lest we contradicted each other's versions.

After such a Godly meal we left after courteous exchanges with a great feeling of love and respect and with our faith in humanity restored. Alok stood out as the hero of the day.

Our stomachs were full, and we had money too... Happy Days Were Here Again.

We broke into a song as we started our walk towards the Siliguri station...

We were happy and merry, we had a spring in our steps, our stomachs were full, and our capital was restored.

We decided to walk to the station and eventually return to base. We were disheveled, dirty, stinking and weary but happy and cheerful. Enquiries revealed a train at around 5 PM which could take us back. We decided to take that by managing the TTE with some money. Being late afternoon, we had enough time and, in the interlude, Vivek ended up making friends with a Sardarji, a senior army man who was travelling with his unit and was to take the same train we had decided upon. The officer soon became friendly with us, introduced us to many of the jawans and also treated us with Tea and snacks. As he was conversing with us, we told him our story which really amused him, and he eventually offered us to travel in the special compartment which was specially booked for the army men.

Since that meant the luxury of free travel, we all agreed.

However, just half an hour before the train arrived Sridip took us all aside and sowed serious doubts in our mind as regards travelling with a bunch of army men. Even when I recount this now, I cannot help but laugh out loud as to how stupid, naive and gullible we were in our thoughts and wisdom.

As per Sridip army men due to their difficult postings and long periods away from their family tended to be lustful and once inside their compartment we were easy prey to their lust. Sridips way of telling and expressing made the narration a stark reality and an impending peril and the more we discussed it the more we believed it and the more it scared us. We finally decided to drop out much to the surprise of the army officer who was urging us to board when the train came in and we were looking the other way and Vivek was trying to explain to him in Punjabi that we wanted to take a later train and so on and so forth.

Finally, when the train chugged out it took our fears away with it and we were left to look at another train which was coming in around 930 PM. We eventually took this night train by managing the TTE at Rs 90/- and settled down at various vantage points inside. We largely fell asleep.

Early morning, we reached Khagra station from where we took cycle rickshaws to the hostel. We reached sometime late in the morning and were quickly surrounded by eager, worried and angry faces. We were missing for three days, and this had set alarm bells ringing. Snehangshu who had left us at Malda had gone back to his native place instead of returning home and the only information the inmates had was through Jhilik who had returned from Siliguri.

The warden took us aside and gave us a piece of his mind, but we could sense that he was relieved on seeing us hale and hearty.

ALL WAS WELL.

Till this day when we friends catch up this trip definitely forms a part of our discussions. It is now a great memory. All the members of this trip have also passed on this incident to their children and by word of mouth this incident lives and breathes as it gets passed through our children to their friends and through us to our friends and acquaintances. Writing it down has been a great and fulfilling experience.

Till date I feel GOD travelled with us too, taking care of us whenever the need arose.

On the way back in the train when we were all stinking at different degrees Saibal and Dhruva had coined a name for each of us relating to the extent and degree of stink of each… I cannot remember the names." Gandhachudamani" was one. I dare not translate it.

Unfortunately, Dhruva is no more. GOD beckoned him too early.

While narrating this I had forgotten that he is no more as he was living in flesh and blood with me through the narrative.

Now the stark reality hits me. RIP… MAN…

My sincere respects to the army men and jawans of India who protect us so that we can live our day.

BUT FOR THE INDIAN RAILWAYS

Genre: Not really a travelogue. Almost a predicament.

It was perhaps the summer of 1978.

Definitely it was summer as Babu could recall that he had been wearing a half shirt and his father was wearing a half shirt too.

No mist was getting formed from exhaled breaths and no one was in woolens.

It was definitely summer.

Sitting in 2018 and thinking of 1978 that is forty years ago was not easy but certain incidents get etched in your memory and when you think of them and travel into the past they unfold like the images in a Kaleidoscope.

They were now unfolding for Babu.

It was leading up to summer vacations and soon the school and the hostel would close for a month. The students were generally happy as their parents would come to pick them up and for a month or so they would enjoy the comfort of home and home food. The hostelers, of course, always wanted to come back soon as the hostel was more fun, and the roving eyes of parents were not always on them. Hostel life pranks and such nuances probably had a greater endearing charm, so punctuations of home stay were fine, but their hearts eventually fell for the hostel life.

On the D Day Babu's father came to pick him up. Babu's father being in the railways had the luxury of a cozy railway rest house whenever he came and Babu along with his bedding and trunk would first normally accompany him to the rest house. There he would take some rest, have a delightful meal attended to by butlers and leave the rest house only minutes before the scheduled time of the train.

Most of the railway men were known to Babu's father and one important ritual was to get a trunk call through to Mom and speak to her and sense the delight in her voice. Her ebullience and happiness would be palpable in the phone itself driven by the news of Babu's home coming for the vacation.

The son was coming home on vacation.

In those days for reaching home Babu had to change trains at a place called Barauni. Father and Babu boarded the train and settled down. The train was scheduled to reach Barauni at around late morning the next day from where they were supposed to change trains for Sonepur.

Babu and his father got down at Barauni only to realize that the connecting train was scheduled to leave in the next five minutes. A coolie was summoned quickly, and they had to make a dash to the other platform. The coolie first, followed by father and Babu. Father got in the compartment followed by the coolie but as Babu was about to get in the train took off. There was a melee at the door as many other people rushed to board and Babu was knocked aside. He watched helplessly as the train sped away, his father inside trying to pull the chain to stop the train, Babu all of 11 years old lost in reverie and struck by nothingness.

Had he discerned a small glint of tear in his father's eyes as the train sped away?

The train was gone and Babu just about 11 years old was suddenly stranded at a railway platform with no clue what to do.

He sauntered down the platform, found a bench and sat down. His mind was blank and in hindsight luckily so as that prevented any sort of action from him.

In the meantime, Father was speeding away in the train which would stop next only at Sonepur three hours away. He was tremendously agitated and constantly thinking of ways to locate and retrieve Babu. Getting down at Sonepur and catching another train back was a matter of seven to eight hours that too if immediate connections were available.

No, he had to activate the railway network.

Meanwhile after sitting on the bench for long Babu fell asleep on the bench. He must have dozed off for at least two hours or more. He was woken up by two gentlemen who were enquiring his name and whereabouts. He was terrified.

He had heard about child trafficking and other such things and withdrew from them giving them a false name and stating that he was waiting for the next train. The gentlemen eventually left. They appeared perplexed but Babu didn't care. He was happy getting rid of them. Considering safety first Babu moved to another bench at another end of the platform and settled himself there. He was fairly ensconced thus when after about fifteen minutes he found the two gentlemen returning, this time with a third gentleman who was quite well dressed and appeared the Senior of the two. This well-dressed man approached Babu held his hand and tugged Babu along. This man looked decent and well-groomed and Babu did not resist.

Along the way this well-dressed man quipped about the other two gentlemen being foolish and irresponsible.

Babu was brought to the Station Masters room and this gentleman turned out to be the Station Master himself. Babu was now relieved. The Station Master placed a trunk call and on connection passed on the receiver to Babu. On the other end was Dad. Dad advised Babu to stay calm and just follow what the Station Master said.

The Station Master ordered some tea and snacks. The next train to Sonepur was due in another half an hour. All arrangements were made and when the train came in Babu was put into the guard's compartment in the custody of the train guards who were advised to handover Babu specifically to Dad at Sonepur.

Dad was eagerly waiting at Sonepur as the train chugged in. Babu was reunited with Dad.

An ordeal thus ended.

What if Dad was not in the railways?

What if the Station Master had not come himself?

What if Babu had sauntered out of the platform and into the city?

40 years and Babu has no answers yet.

But for the Indian Railways…

PASSING OF A SOUL FORETOLD – A CHRONICLE

Genre: Obituary along the timeline

It was the winter of 2004. It was early January.

The city of Kolkata however was not famous for its severe winters and the winter of 2004 was not different. It was cold enough for the elderly, pleasant enough for the young, just about enough to bring out sweaters and shawls and allow picnickers to revel.

There was no profuse sweating, no killing humidity, no garrulous rainfall. It was the season of book fairs, film festivals, weekend breaks. The biriyani was easier digested and hot chocolates made a comeback. The morning sun was soothing to the body and Christmas had just got over having handed the baton to the new year and having added another calendar year to the Doctor's life.

The day before the death Doctor Mitra felt fine. In the morning he sat at the lovely balcony of his house, read the newspaper, and sipped on to his tea. The morning sunbathed him and caressed him. He felt nice and cozy. He had a shawl draped around him. His conventional dark greyish shawl which made him feel warm. Inspite of his weakening heart and his age of 84 he loved this morning ritual at the balcony of his two storied house.

Many a passerby in the street below wished him and he exchanged pleasantries with them.

Dr Saha was a regular" late morning" walker. At his age of 79 he felt no need to rush early into his morning walk. 7.30 AM was a good time for him to leave and return by about 8.30 AM or so. The day before the death he started off in his usual round and route. Stopping once below the balcony of Dr Mitra, as was his routine. This day too he shouted out to Dr Mitra." Hello Doctor Mittir, what are the headlines for today". "Nothing new," said Dr Mitra. "Some news on Vote on Account, one of the coldest winters reported at Kokkata @ 9.4 degrees" went on Dr Mitra. " Yes, this winter is colder" agreed Dr Saha. They then chatted for a while and then Dr Saha went ahead with his morning walk and Dr Mitra continued with his newspaper reading.

The day before the death Mrs Mitra got up early.She always got up early. She had to make tea for Doctor Mitra and for her eldest son Babu. She would follow it up with breakfast preparations. She decided on *Luchi* and *subzi* for breakfast. In any case Dr Mitra had wanted to have *Luchi* and *subzi* today.

She was a bit reluctant because she thought that such deep-fried preparation was perhaps not good for Dr Mitra's heart, but she fought the reluctance back with the thought of allowing the old man, who had always enjoyed his food, his choice of food. More so, as she felt that she could pack the same for her elder son Babu towards his office lunch. That saved her the arduous task of trying to make something else for Babu and in any case Babu liked *Luchi* for his office lunch pack too.

The day before the death the elder son Babu went about his own routine of getting up, having his tea, quick breakfast, bath, pick up his lunch box and rush to office. He and his friend Chandan, also his neighbor, took the 8 AM Chartered bus together. To the bus stop from the house was a five-minute brisk walk. Chandan as usual walked faster than Babu and Babu was always trying to keep pace with him. The bus was on time and once settled inside the bus Babu's thoughts veered to the pending tasks at office. There were two important claim files to be attended to, there was a discussion on the structure of the presentation to be made to a client and so on.

The day before the death the younger son Bunti had to rush to the factory at odd hours to attend to a breakdown. His job location being far away from Kolkata he always made it a point to call his parents Dr Mitra and Mrs Mitra daily. He particularly would check on his father who had survived two mild heart attacks in the past. However today was different. The breakdown at the plant was serious and he realized he would have a long day perhaps spilling over deep into the night.

Dr Mitra finished reading the newspaper and strolled in from the balcony to enjoy his breakfast which he ate with great satisfaction post which he opened his file of investments to review them and later in the afternoon decided to walk down to the bank near his house for some work.

Dr Saha in the meantime had gone to his chamber to attend to his patients. Dr Mrs Roy a gynecologist and neighbor of Dr Mitra had a Caesarian to attend to and she was preparing herself for the OT.

Mrs Mitra was supervising the maids and preparing for lunch, Babu had just made an office note on the first claim file and put it up to his manager for approval, Bunti was inside the plant giving directions to his foreman. The breakdown had halted production and it was important to get the plant up and running soon. Chandan had a lot to attend in office and was busy.

The afternoon before the death was thus mundane in nature. There was nothing unusual about the afternoon. No storm, no rain, no hail, no breaking news. Nothing really to disturb the routine.

After lunch Dr Mitra had his medicines and settled into his Siesta. Before he did that, he spent some time reading a novel. He was nearing the end and the suspense leading up to the climax was intriguing him. He decided to leave the last chapter for the morrow. Going into siesta thinking of the climax, which was still unknown, was, as per him, the readers' delight.

Mrs Mitra was winding up her work for the day, organizing and cleaning the kitchen. She too loved her afternoon nap. It was a much-needed rest from the din and bustle of activity of the morning.

Soon the afternoon dissolved into evening and Dr Mitra settled down to watch TV, Dr Saha was getting ready for a family get together, Chandan and Babu had started back home from office, the breakdown at the plant was taken care of but Bunti decided to stay on till normalcy of production returned, Mrs Mitra was relaxing at the balcony waiting for her son to arrive back from office after which her chores would again begin.

The night before the death it was all quiet at the Mitra household. Dinner was laid out at 10 PM just after Dr Mitra had had an early dinner. Mita Babu's wife had also served early dinner to the two kids who had been sent off to sleep. The kids were too young and early to bed was the norm for them as set by Mita. Mita, Babu and Mrs Mitra then sat down for dinner. The talk at the dinner table was as usual a bit about everything, a bit about the kids, a bit about Bunti, a bit about Dr Mitra's health… a bit about everything really. Finally, they all retired for the day and the Mitra household had gone into slumber for the night.

Dr Mitra felt that the night was slightly colder as he needed two blankets that day. He checked the usual things by his bed side. A glass of water, sorbitrate tablets, his pullover which he would need as he got up in the morning and his slippers just below the bed.

Chandan got the phone call at 7.30 the next morning and rushed.

Mita had rushed to Dr Mrs Roy at 7.35 the next morning. She rushed too.

Bunti got the call around 8.00 AM and rushed to his home to plan for the immediate journey to Kolkata.

Dr Saha during his usual morning walk found the balcony empty and rushed in.

Mrs Mitra had discovered him lying in the bathroom and thought he had fallen. She rushed to call her son Babu who was having a bath.

When Mita was back with Dr Mrs Roy she heard Mrs Mitra scream and rushed.

Babu cut short his bath and rushed out.

Dr Mitra had got up at his usual time. He had his glass of water, got out of his bed, wore his pullover, took the sorbitrate tablet wrapper in his hand and went into the bathroom to wash his face and brush his teeth.

Inside the bathroom he felt a numbness and a pressure on his chest. Being a doctor himself he had an inkling. He tore upon the tablet wrapper and fell to the floor littering the tablets all around him.

Babu found him on the bathroom floor and tried to pump his heart. He also quickly called Chandan.

But it was late. The SOUL HAD PASSED AWAY

OM SHANTI OM

Genre: Close to the heart obituary.

News of deaths are not infrequent in today's world. Many die every day around the world and many of these deaths don't move us and even those that move us do so momentarily, after all we are human beings and we do feel sad about say a bus accident, a terrorist bombing killing innocents and so on and so forth.

We all know that while life may be uncertain the only certainty that comes complimentary with life is death.

Even then there come deaths which shake us badly and shake us to the very core.

18th of September 2018 was one such day.

I was in office and into a meeting when Ratan Sengupta, an old and senior ex colleague of mine, called me. Being in a meeting I was unable to take the call. It was then that Ratan da texted me and I reproduce the language of the text verbatim:

"Achintya Mallik Passed way today morning at Mumbai"

My return call to Ratan da and a few more colleagues/ex colleagues/friends confirmed the news.

On the fateful day Achintya went through his usual morning routine, had breakfast, packed his lunch and left for office. He took an auto from Hiranandani Gardens, Powai to the Kanjur Marg station (from where he would board the train for office), stepped out of the auto and collapsed.

The auto driver and a few passersby propped him up by the roadside and used his mobile to make a few calls on the basis of last few numbers dialed, and the speed of technology carried the news through calls, texts and whatsapp messages everywhere.

The time of death could have been around 8.55 AM or so maybe 9.00 AM. At around 8.45 AM he had sent the following whatsapp message in his friends' group. Perhaps the last communication of his life.

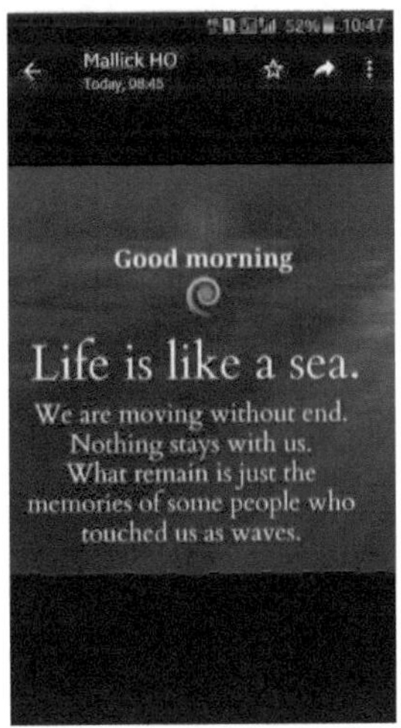

His colleagues from National Insurance Mumbai rushed to the spot, retrieved him and carried him to the Hirandani Hospital where he was declared **"Brought Dead".**

At 56 a life had come to an end sending tremors of sadness among friends and foes (He had none) and leaving the family devastated.

I perhaps met him for the first time in the year 1996 and was not impressed at first sight. Here was a boy in very simple attire who hardly spoke, always smiled at anything and everything and seemed to be too casual about his demeanor and gait. He did not fit in my own *muddle-headed* description of an officer.

Gradually we became personal friends first, family friends later and realized how wrong and in-accurate my first impression had been. Hiding behind the shadows of what I just described was a highly intelligent, calm and composed human being. A person who was an Aeronautical Engineer from IIT, highly efficient and capable at his work, had not the slightest airs about anything, could smile away even at the very tense of situations and who was always eager to help anyone and everyone.

What amazed me was the purity of his heart and intentions and his uncanny ability to face any situation in office or personal life with a calmness of composure and a patent smile that went on to become a hallmark of Achintya.

In many of my trying situations in life just his presence beside me had always been a great pacifier.

His wife Rakhi would always jocularly tell my wife that they were a unique husband and wife who never had a fight. You know why..............No matter what happened and no matter how angry Rakhi was Achintya would never fight back, never utter a word, never try to defend himself and in his own hallmark style just stay calm and silent with that patent smile of his hanging on his lips. In the absence of fuel, therefore. the fight would die at birth or get nipped in the bud.

Many a times I even thought that this was perhaps the only grievance Rakhi had about her husband that she never succeeded in engaging him in a heated argument or debate.

Once my father fell seriously ill and was hospitalized. The situation was serious as he was passing blood with his urine. I had decided to stay at the hospital but the situation being tense I needed company. I called Achintya and he was there in a jiffy. He spent two days and two nights at the hospital and every night we would sleep together on the floor and get up to attend to my father when required. During these two nights my father kept passing blood with his urine and as advised by the doctor we would collect my father's urine in bottles for testing the next day.

During those days Achintya was like my own brother helping me to collect the urine without any sense of disgust or disdain. His mere presence was soothing enough to make me believe that my father would come out of this and come out he did.

I walked out of the hospital not only with my father but also with a sense of great respect for this man. Whenever I have thought of him the one image that would always cross my mind was his presence at the hospital beside me. Even as I write this, I can visualize the hospital room with my father on the hospital bed and Achintya and me in the room on the floor trying to catch up with some sleep.

In those days, mid-nineties, he would smoke a lot — a habit which he discarded in a couple of years. Most of the times I would borrow cigarettes from him and on many occasions out of the pack of ten I would end up smoking Seven/eight leaving only three/two for Achintya. One day he told me, jokingly of course, that he would calculate the number of cigarettes I took from him and find out the monthly amount which I was blowing away at his expense. Not to be let down by this I retorted back saying that he should consider himself lucky that I left for him the two or three cigarettes which should be accounted as his savings.

This was a cause of much laughter amongst us, and the joke went around our office and our colleagues too and many would actually pull Achintya's leg saying that I was actually ensuring a savings for him instead of an expense.

He lived his life in a very simple way. Extravagance, the lure of consumerism and brands never touched him. He spent what was needed, made no compromises on his spending when required and at the same time was never an extravagant or an impulsive spender.

I have seen him struggle with his finances in a big way when he decided to buy an apartment at Kolkata. He surrendered all his Life Insurance Policies, channelized his savings, took a House Building Loan from the Company and bought a small flat at Garia, Kolkata. The flat was small, short of space but abounding in love and hospitality. Whenever we went to the flat both Achintya and Rakhi would go overboard to ensure that we were comfortable, felt at home and that we never left without a very fulfilling and wholesome meal.

I never heard him complain about anything. Not even about his job. Many a times I thought that God had forgotten to put the word complaint into his being. He was as comfortable in an overcrowded bus or train as he was in a limousine. He could happily sleep on the floor in the absence of a bed, and I gradually realized that life could never disturb him, definitely not on the outside. If there was some disturbance or turmoil inside it never came out.

He was a great father and a great family man too. He brought up his son in the most practical way possible and Guddu eventually went on to study at Ramakrishna Mission Narendrapur, Jadavpur University and eventually went abroad to Spain, France and Germany for his higher studies. I met him after long recently following the demise and he had blossomed into a man of 24. He appeared calm, quiet and composed as well, a trait which I am sure got passed onto him from Achintya and Rakhi.

Achintya was proud of his son, and you could sense the pride whenever he spoke about Guddu. I am sure he did not speak about Guddu much to many people. It was not his habit to talk about the accomplishments of his son. When he spoke about Guddu to me he would always refer to Guddu as ***"Shriman"*** and this world echoes in the hollow recesses of my memory now.

He bought another flat at New Town, Kolkata and a big one this time, a 3 BHK Flat and proudly took me one day to show me the flat during its construction stage. The slabs were casted, and the construction was on. He felt happy and relieved to have eventually managed to buy a decent sized flat. He would have never known then that in future he would not be there to enjoy the flat he so proudly acquired.

Quite some time ago when he was posted at Dumka he had met with a serious accident but pulled through it. He was transferred to Mumbai recently and stayed for long at the guest house. Eventually took up a Company Flat at Powai and shifted Rakhi only recently (just about 20/25/35 days before his death).

They had both called us and it was their desire that this year we celebrate the Durga Puja at Mumbai together. My wife told Rakhi that she should now enjoy her life without tension as Guddu was doing well with his Doctorate abroad and so on and so forth. Rakhi said who knew what tension the future brings. None of us knew then that in the very immediate future Achintya would just drop dead in the most bizaare way and in the untimeliest fashion.

As a group, ex colleagues and friends from National we had met a few months back at a club at Mumbai. Organised by Bhaskar and Sumona. We had a wonderful evening and dinner together. Bhaskar, Subhankar, Amitabh, Sumona, Achintya and yours truly.

While this group in their fifties was largely discussing about retired life and pension Achintya was talking about getting transferred to another city in a few years which would allow him to savour in the flavour of another city of India as a part of his job.

The entire team of National pitched in to support on hearing about his death. Everything from the postmortem to the funeral was handled by colleagues and friends who loved him. They stood firm, they consoled, and they cried. They continued to be around trying to help the family through this phase of crisis.

The body was brought to the Cremation Ground at Vikhroli and laid supine on the slab. It was decorated and embellished with flowers, garlands, incense and smeared with Ghee. What an Irony. The man who shied away from public glare and all sorts of embellishments in life was decorated, embellished and garlanded in death.

I could not muster up the courage to look at the body. However, there is one thing I am sure of, that even in death just as in life, his lips would still have been curved up in that patent smile of his.

During the three days after the death, Rakhi would cling to my wife and cry. She kept hoping against hope that Achintya might just call or might just ring the bell and walk in. She held my hand and spoke

"Is he really gone". I couldn't reply because I was not sure if he was really gone. He seemed all around me with his inimitable smile.

Achintya knew Rakhi since she was in class XI. They had an affair and a marriage. One fine morning Achintya just walked up to Rakhi and said, "Let's get married tomorrow". This simple girl from the suburbs of Kolkata just obliged and thereby began a journey of togetherness "In Filmy Style" says Rakhi…… looks blank, drops a tear or two and speaks

"He passed way in Filmy Style too is it not"

We did not have an answer again.

When I left Kolkata, we were not in regular touch with Achintya and Rakhi.

He kept a tab of my whereabouts, my life, my children and so did I. For all these years I have been trying to find one moment when Achintya was angry or had a fight. I haven't yet been able to find one. All those who happen to read this and who also knew Achintya to them I say… *I am looking for a single moment when he was angry and shouting and fighting. If you find any such a moment do let me know…*

There are many memories, many incidents and recounting all of them would take up a lifetime.

Achintya very soon we will join you. We have to because that is the certainty of life. Friends and Foes (did you have any?) alike. We will meet again and we will start again like the inimitable smile which never left you, like the candle and the wind, like the rubber flip flops which you used to wear, like the wills navy cut packets, like the home that you built brick by brick with layers and layers of love and caring, like the car that you bought like the book on Aviation Insurance that you wrote but never gave me a copy, like the fried fish you ordered for me when I visited you in office.

There was a gathering long overdue. Subroto and Mallika, Joydeep, Suman, Debasish and Dolly, Me and Paramita, You and Rakhi.

There was so much of life left in you. How could you just leave mate? How could you just throw away your wicket? There are many more overs to go and many more runs to make. I look up from the non-Strikers' end but don't see you. I look all around and don't see you. You have already walked into the Pavillion and disappeared.

I am blank, I am stranded at the non-Strikers end, I look at the horizon and hope for bad light……… at least for now.

In Hinduism we believe in the ***passing away of the soul*** and in the cycle of death and rebirth till we attain Moksha. Will Achintya be reborn? I don't know. Will Achintya attain Moksha? I don't know. Will I hear is voice again? I know I won't…

Agni Dahe na Jare (That which fire cannot burn)

Shastre chende na jare (That which weapons cannot pierce)

Na Hanyate ayee Hanyaman Sharire (Immortal in this mortal body)

P.S: The obituary written by friends is reproduced below.

In Remembrance

QUOTE

It is said that good men are so loved by God, they get called to the heavens earlier.

Mr Achintya Mallick (6th December 1962 – 18th September 2018) was a great employee, a better father, and a best friend to many.

Mallick Da, as he was fondly called, will always be remembered for his soft, humble nature, which gracefully hid the sheer volume of talent and knowledge he held. Nobody ever saw him scold anyone, no matter how grave a crime or insubordination someone committed. He always had a way of getting people to turn around, find a better path, and love their life. And he always did it with a smile on his face.

While nothing can ever fill the void left behind by him, we vow to carry forward his legacy and his teachings, so that the world can be blessed with more people who think, and care like him.

We pray for his soul to rest in peace, and hope that his family is able to cope with this untimely accident…

Our deepest condolences are with his family…

With heartfelt sorrow:

FRIENDS

UNQUOTE

HARATHI NIMESHAATH KAALA SARVAM

Genre: Close to the heart obituary II, Achintya's Obituary continued

Almost 12 days have rolled by since Achintya left for his divine abode and most of us have returned to our daily chores and normal life.

I am Time……

I am Time, I do not wait for anyone. I cannot stop, I cannot be stopped. I just flow from the past to the present to the future.

The piece that I wrote on Achintya evoked responses from many friends, colleagues, acquaintances and I am sure each one of us who wrote about Achintya could visualize him while doing so. The all-pervading Achintya would have been with all of us who wrote about him. There are many who also responded to me on whatsapp instead of writing at the site.

I am Time……

On that day on which I wrote the piece on Achintya I had woken up early with a lot of chatter in my mind. Everything about Achintya had been coming back to me and taking up its own space in my mind and many of them moving down to the heart.

It was a difficult moment.

I realized that I had to get it out.

Therefore, I started writing about Achintya and I wrote in a trance till the mind had settled down and I could breathe easy and think easy.

I am Time……

Many called it "A wonderful Obituary"but it was not meant to be an Obituary at all. I could not have written an Obituary on Achintya.

As Suman Ganguly wrote ***"We are all Achintya". "I can still hear him laugh… Ha … Ha… Ha"***

How can there be an obituary?

Many people wrote a lot of things about Achintya and I would sit and read all that everyone had written Once, twice, thrice, many times. He was there, he was laughing……he was everywhere……………

I am Time………..

It would be apt for me to now create the essence of Achintya through the thoughts, feelings,and emotions of everyone.

1. Humility was definitely one aspect of Achintya everyone talked about. His feet never left the ground and that is why perhaps he leaves his footprints.

2. The simplicity of his thoughts and his calmness and composure stood out to everybody. He just took it in his stride.

3. He led his life devoid of conflicts and chose to be humane and just not human.

4. He always seemed eager to help all and sundry. The helping hand was always kept extended for anyone who wanted to hold it.

5. He carried no rancor.

6. Most of us did re-visit his evergreen smile breaking through the barriers of life. The smile that stuck to him as if it was embedded into him.

7. His intelligence shone to everybody and many thought that his potential remained largely unutilized.

8. There was lot of mention of his hospitality too.

Specially for the family and for many it started with shock and disbelief and from there to belief and thereby to acceptance and then grief settled in...... But time intervened...

I am Time……

The past moved on to the present and to the future. Anon and Yonder and the distant thunder no matter what they bring, time steps in, lifts you up and carries you away into the future, there is no wait, no halt just a journey… **I am time**… I will transpose you and not leave you in your present and / or in your past…

Time is the best healer. It will heal for the family too.

However, there will come moments when Achintya comes back in talks and discussions and the mind will go back in time… For the Wife and the Son Achintya will keep coming back even though time will keep pulling them into the future.

I am Time……

The ways colleagues and friends have stood up and continue to do so has been commendable. The least one can do is to hold the hands of the bereaved family and walk them into the future and allow time to heal.

The Son will go back to his studies and one day meet his calling. He shall blossom into a fine young man and do well in life and everyone through him would again see Achintya. More so Rakhee for whom the blooming of Arijit into Achintya would be for her a home coming, a return to the past…

And somewhere in the firmament a star will twinkle brighter, and we will know who that star is……God knows some day when we keep looking at the sky the Star might just smile back at us...............

But I am Time...............

Sunset and evening star
And one clear call for me!
And may there be no moaning of the bar,
When I put out to sea,
But such a tide as moving seems asleep,
Too full for sound and foam,
When that which drew from out the boundless deep
Turns again home.
Twilight and evening bell,
And after that the dark!
And may there be no sadness of farewell,
When I embark.
For though from out our bourne of Time and Place
The flood may bear me far,
I hope to see my Pilot face to face
When I have crossed the bar.

(Poem by Alfred Tennyson)

RELATIONSHIPS HAVE THEIR TASTE TOO

Genre: Food and Relationships and Memories

I once saw a Whatsapp Video which spoke about the ***"Tastes of Relationship".***

It was an interesting video which very nicely linked Relationships to certain lingering tastes.

The person spoke about his father in a small-time job, who, once in a while on his way back from office, would save money to bring him "Samosas" (*Samosas are a triangular savory pastry fried in ghee or oil containing spiced vegetable)* wrapped in News Papers.

This taste, it seems, lingered on after his death and the son would recall as to how affectionately his father would bring home these samosas for his him. Among the various memories of his father, this was one memory which stuck with him.

I had tears in my eyes when I saw this video.

So that set me thinking and I have been able to discover a plethora of tastes in my various relationships.

Some living, some gone, some in touch, some out of touch but when you think of it there is a taste to the relationship which stays with you.

Should we call it the "Essence of Relationships"?

Period: 1972 through to 1983.

I had my Nanihal at Bhagalpur. *Emphasis on the word had.* The house has been sold off long ago.

For those who don't know "Nani" is Maternal Grandmother and the place where she would live was/ is called the "Nanihal". Interesting that this word derives from the Feminine Form and not given to the oft practiced gender bias- being called after the Nani and not the Nana (Paternal Grandfather).

The house at Bhagalpur was called the "Happy Villa", It was a biggish two storey house with a lovely garden and lawn at the front and a wonderful courtyard on the inside. The rooms, the kitchen, the storeroom was lined around the perimeter of the courtyard. The courtyard had a nice tubewell at one corner and a Tulsi Tree (Basil Leaf Tree) at one end. The sunshine would bathe the open courtyard and in winters it used to be a lovely place to recline on an armchair and enjoy the sun.

My Grandmother would spend, as would most housewives in those days, a lot of time in the kitchen. You could always smell the various aromas that would emanate from this sanctum sanctorum of hers. The cooking was elaborate, and meals were a well spread-out family affair. There are certain tastes that linger about her.

The "Hing Kachoris" (Fluffy round shaped deep fried Indian bread with an essence of Asafoetida) were her specialty and they would be served with a lovely potato curry and would make up for a lovely breakfast. Every bite of it would carry the lovely aroma of the hing and the hot crispy crunch of the Kachori.

I can even smell it even now and feel the taste of it as I write. There were other tastes about her too. The taste of "Puli Pithas" (A traditional Bengali sweet of steamed rice dumplings) usually eaten with a viscous melt of date jaggery.

She is no more and amongst the various memories she also lives through these tastes and also takes you back to the lovely house with its own crevices and corners and smells and the ever-cheery Grandfather who loved his food.

Period: 1975 to 1981

Long years of my life have been spent in hostels. St Xaviers – A Christian Missionary School to start with. I distinctly recall the Principal, Father Anthony Gatt with his Havanna Cigars and his pet Alsatian.

The smell of the Cigar and the smell of the dog would precede his arrival and in that order.

Hostel food has always been in all hostels the most vivacious topic. No exception to this here. However, the taste that lingers is that of the brownish pooris (An Indian deep fried bread) which were served twice a week and the mutton curry which was served once a week. The brown pooris had a particular aroma and you could smell their cooking from the morning itself. The mutton had a typical taste too. Boarders of that era, if they happen to read this would surely be able to smell it and feel the taste of it even today. Not to forget the sumptuous meals on hostel days…

Period: 1981 to 1983.

Moving on "Ramakrishna Mission Residential College" with its vast expanse and the hostel block "Bramha" had its own taste. I recall the "Moori and Bonde" served as evening snacks along with tea. The hosteliers would carry their own plate and stand in queue for the helping of this snack. (Bonde – Indian dessert made from sweetened, fried chickpea flour. (Moori-Puffed rice commonly used as a breakfast cereal or snack food).

I also recall the fusion whiff of various foods brought by parents on weekends as they came to visit their wards.

Period 1983 to 1987

Fast Forward to the engineering college hostel at Behrampore, West Bengal. So many memories and so many tastes.

I distinctly recall "Thakurmoshai" (The Chief Cook / Main Chef) cooking with his lungi (A wrap dress worn around the waist) and his vest and stirring away with his ladle.

He was a chain smoker and smoked beedis (Local cigarette made of unprocessed tobacco wrapped in leaves) and the smell of the Beedi permeated itself through the kitchen into the dining hall. The taste of his watery dal (lentil soup) and his chicken curry do filter through even now.

Regular days were on cheap budgets save the once in a month GF (Grand Feast) day and the same lungi clad beedi smoking, naïve cook would churn up various delicacies and the festivities and their taste would traverse long into the night.

The Behrampore town, largely a sleepy hamlet in those days" has / had its own food and the tastes of "Sar Rooti" (Bread laced with burnt sugar and milk cream) and "Chana Bada" (A roundish dark fried milk based sweet meat dipped in sugar syrup) seep in.

My mother has been a great cook herself. She carried forward the tradition of her mother and also many of her recipes. With time she evolved her own recipes and mixed and matched various recipes to create a taste of her own. She would also spend a long time in the kitchen and at one point of time cooked all alone for nine people each of whom had their own likings and disliking about various foods, different times for meals and various favourites.

She managed it all.

The cherry on the cake surely was her light gravy, Mutton Curry. Sundays used to be Mutton Day and every Sunday we would all wake up with the thought of a lovely afternoon meal replete with Mutton curry and rice along with a bit of salad and fries of some kind. My Father had his own style of savouring this mutton curry. The Mutton curry for him would be laid out on a large glass plate/rice plate. There would essentially be a half potato embellishing the gravy and father would eat it with great delight and ebullience enjoying the light gravy with a tablespoon and licking his taste buds till the last morsel.

My father loved his "karaisuti Kachoris" (A puri stuffed with mashed spiced up peas) too.

The smell of these Kachoris while being fried was an Olfactory delight.

The smell of Mutton undergoing the process of cooking would start enveloping the house from around 11.30 AM as it would get cooked and before Mom would eventually put all the contents into the pressure cooker for the final round, I would essentially pick up a piece (a bit uncooked) and some gravy and enjoy it with bread or two. A sort of preview to the final meal.

Other tastes about her have been some more of her specialties. The cake baked at home, the lovely "Dahi Vadas" (Prepared by soaking fried flour balls in thick yoghurt), the pudding and the custard.

Father is no more now. Wherever he is I am sure he is not missing his Sunday Mutton as my mother no more cooks, except very occasionally but when she does, she always places the first serving in front of the photograph of my father.

The first taste thus is still his……

Two of my friends passed away in two separate tragic incidents. Vijay Benwal a colleague of mine when I was in National Insurance was a chirpy, vivacious, "heart in his sleeve" guy. Came up from a village in Uttar Pradesh and a carried of a lot of the rural charm, rituals and hospitality.

His family was a crowd as he had four daughters, one son, his wife, his sister and his mother all living in the same house. In those bachelor days me and my friend Himanshu Sharma (Sometimes we would also have Neeraj, Vinay and Ram join in but I and Himanshu were the regulars). Vijay's wife would cook for us and her large chapatis laced with butter were a special attraction. We would sit on the floor in the kitchen and eat away. The smell of the thick large chapati emanating from the kitchen and served with either Lentils and/or mutton/ chicken curry was a favourite taste.

Vijay Benwal passed away in his prime following a massive heart attack.

Surinder another colleague died out of a road accident leaving behind a cute little daughter and his almost newlywed wife.

He was very fond of his namkeen (Salty and Savoury snack) and would bring large packets for us from his hometown of Jabalpur.

My wife Paramita kept learning and improving her cooking style along the way. Experimenting with her own recipes she kept on inventing and making certain delicacies of her own. The friends of our kids, today, love her cooking and frequently drop into our house to enjoy a bite of it.

Largely on demand are her Chicken Curry (In various styles), the chicken kebabs, the egg kebab (a process of making which she sort of discovered on her own). She also is good with her cake, pudding and custard. Her "Chaler Payesh" (A rice pudding made by boiling rice with milk) made out of Date Jaggery is the " top of mind recall' or the lingering taste.

The Payesh creates its own aroma while being cooked and so does her mutton curry. The Egg Kebab hides its aroma until it hits your palate.

I and my younger daughter recall the taste of her Mutton Curry while my elder daughter recalls the taste and aroma of her grilled chicken.

Let me now recall certain people and link them to taste.

My friend Sayantani's Dhania Mutton (Dhania – Coriander), My sister in law Tumpa's Prawn Malai Curry, The baked "Bhetki" (A particular variety of fish

) of my "Maima" (Aunt in law), The Mutton cooked by Shantanu in his own style, The quintessential Bengali dishes of Chandrima and Dolon, the Idlis, Dosais and Vadas of Jayashree, Sudha, Vizy and Ram.

The Kachoris and Namkeens of Allahabad brought for me by my sister and her Dahi Vadas.

We spent quite some time in Gurgaon. Our family friend Sunita brought in a lot of her taste too. Especially the "Aaaloo and Muli Parathas" (Flatbreads made with a stuffing of Potato and Radish) and also Methi Parathas (Flatbreads made with Fenugreek Leaves). The Kamal Kakdi Subzi (Lotus root vegetable) had its own flavour and taste.

My daughter Sanya loves her Pasta, and my younger daughter Khushi loves her Garlic Bread, my wife Paramita loves her Jalebis (An Indian sweet made of a coil of batter fried and steeped in hot sugar syrup). These are the tastes that go with them.

My Father-in-Law is a Health Freak and a disciplined eater so to say. I can associate him with his typical fish curry – largely a light gravy and his "Chana" (Cheese curd made from regular milk by adding food acids).

My Mother In-law's Cashew Paneer vegetable (An Indian Cottage Cheese Vegetable) is a tasty delight.

These tastes get linked to them.

We once travelled to Ostrava, a small town in the Czech Republic, where my brother and his family stay now. We spent a few days at their house. My Sister-In-law made some wonderful dishes. The taste of the Lamb Curry hangs on and so does the taste of the smoothie. There were other tastes too but since we ate a lot outside, we need to make another visit to identify more tastes.

Niranjan was our Bungalow Peon when my father was in the Railways. Niranjan moved on to become part of our household and addressed my mother as mother too.

A great human being with great culinary skills he churned up various recipes for us. I recall the days when we would sit around the earthen oven and eat while he cooked for us.

Most of his dishes stood out with special mention of his chicken curry, his sweetmeats, his chicken and mutton pulao and so on.

I can feel the taste of each of these relationships and I am sure as I continue further into my life's journey more relationships with their own tastes will keep getting added.

There have been and are many more relationships with their own tastes and I would probably have to plan a sequel to this.

Quickly recalling "Mantu da" the street vendor in front of National Insurance Head Office at Kolkata.

Many from National Insurance and / or otherwise would recall Mantu Da.

I leave them with their own taste of Mantu Da.

I am sure to have missed out on certain tastes and obviously certain relationships linked with them in this piece.

MOTHER OH MOTHER

Genre: Ode, Compiled and Collected and Reproduced

My Mother never understood mathematics.

When I asked for one bread, she gave me two.

When I asked for Rupees 20 to go out with friends, she gave me 50.

My Mother never understood English.

When I told her "I hate you".

She loved me more.

My Mother was a liar.

When she did not eat, she said she did.

Even when she was hungry, she saved my favourite foods for me.

My Mother was Foolish.

Throughout her life she toiled in the kitchen

And kept bothering about our likes and dislikes.

My Mother was a Thief.

She stole money from my father's wallet to give to me.

She pilfered my favourite eats from picnics she attended.

My Mother was Shameless.

I told her many times not to touch my things

But she kept organizing my untidy and unkempt room.

My Mother had no common sense.

Whenever she saw food less on my plate, she would fill it up.

Even after I ate a lot, she thought I was hungry.

My Mother was careless.

She hid her pains and niggles and never took her medicines.

But she turned the world upside down calling doctors and hospitals even if I coughed a little.

My Mother was un-smart.

She never wore costly dresses and never spent on herself.

She only thought of making me smart.

My Mother was selfish.

She could sacrifice everything on earth for her husband and her children.

My Mother was perhaps the worst person in the world.

That is why we children gave her so much trouble.

That is why we never cared for her much…

She was Mom just Mom.

(A Compilation and Translation from an unknown source)

SACCHU DA – THE OFFICER

Genre: Satire, Comedy, Humour

Indore in the late 80s and early 90s was a quaint little town.

It was not a village, nor was it semi urban, it was urban + so to say where the shades and effects of large cities of India were trickling in more in the construction and physical developmental activity rather than in the minds of people.

The young ***Indorean*** was thus a fusion of the past and the present. An amalgamation of old values and neo spirit and neo thoughts.

He/She was replacing the typical ***Indori*** Hindi with punctuations of English, developing a greater liking for the cinema than their previous generation, going to pubs and bars, getting into a different dress sense, buying jazzy motor bikes, looking to date and become outward, study in convents, eat in restaurants on weekends and talk of the world.

Into this interesting city with its ***Chatris and Sarafas*** was born Sacchu da. Well not much about his childhood and early life need be recounted here as we are going to fast forward to the era when he was all of 59 years of age (just a year shy of his retirement) and an officer in a Public Sector Company.

He was the quintessential clerk turned officer by long practice and by dint of seniority. He was the amalgamation of the Indore of the past and the present. He was the cantilever bridge with one end of his support in the past during his clerical days and the other end in the present age of his so-called ***officer-ship***. At that time, he was an Assistant Manager which meant that he had been an officer for at least 12 to 13 years and cherished the ***officer-ship*** a great deal in the process realizing that officers needed to behave and carry themselves in a different way as compared to clerks and so called other lesser mortals and had thus imbibed certain styles of behavior and demeanor which Sacchu da thought to be ***officer like***.

For example, his hair would be neatly dyed black, his shoes would have a perfect shine, his shirt and pant would be well pressed and ironed, he would call for his tea only at pre-defined intervals and that too by **ringing the bell on his table by thumping on it thrice,**

The Great Bell of Sacchu

refuse to sign documents which he thought were unworthy of an officer of his caliber, maintain a straight serious face, speak in English most of the time and carry his punctuality to the T, dictate letters loudly,largely to indicate his command over English, instead of writing them (which was the common practice then and very ***Un Officer*** like according to him) thereby causing people to stop work and listen and suppress their laughter as his English did not really follow the queen's lineage, pull out his fork and spoon to have his lunch alone during office hours, ask ***officer like questions*** on matters brought to his table, use a pencil to underline things which need not have been underlined, look up around him, once in a while, with a condescending eye to the large group of non-officers in front of him and so on and so forth.

He always felt that one should look and behave like an officer. To the others, of course, he became a character straight out of a comic book and thus was the joke of the office and many a joke about him circulated in office even leaning to his propensity of trying to make passes at young girls (Because Sacchu da was an officer carrying a distinct pedigree, young at heart and thought he looked very young too) and asking them out for dates. Of course, the girls always thought of him as their uncle and played along adding to the fun, frolic and leg pulling that kept happening egregiously behind him and subtly in front of him.

He was fun for us too.

Himanshu, Neeraj,Vinay, Surender,Myself, Vijay, Ram, Terrence, Sandip would often talk about him and would often have a laugh or two at his expense. Himanshu many a times would go and sit with Sacchu da and engage him in English and thereby making a stage for us to watch a comedy in action.

Sacchu da however liked us perhaps more because he thought we were **Direct Officers** and thereby to some extent up his alley and league. He had a subtle disdain for the clerical cadre and so by default we were in his so-called good books.

Therefore, when Sacchu Da's daughter was to get married we – meaning Himanshu, Neeraj, Myself, Vinay, Sandip got invited. He gave the wedding card to Himanshu, neatly wrote the names of all of us on the envelope and requested us all to come for the wedding.

Now wedding those days for us (we were all bachelors then) was more about good food for free at somebody else's expense and we looked at this marriage no differently. On the day of the marriage, we decided to go together on our two wheelers. The plan was to have a nice meal, quickly eat and leave and catch up with some movie playing at the night show.

Surender, a movie buff, was with us that day and though not invited he decided to join us and crash into the marriage as well (not a very uncommon practice with us bachelors during those days). On reaching the marriage venue we parked our scooters outside only to be told by Neeraj that courtesy demanded that we should all contribute, put the contribution in an envelope and hand over to the bride. Well, this was met with some resistance because that would put a cost to our free food, but Neeraj prevailed upon us and lo and behold we were rushing to the nearby stationery store to buy an envelope. That done there was a loud debate on how much to contribute beginning with Rs 10/-. It was eventually decided that we contribute Rs 250/- each (Not too bad an amount in those days). The amount of Rs 1250/- was neatly put in the envelope (Surender was gate crashing so ethically no contribution was taken from him but only after extracting a promise from him that after the movie he would treat us to ice cream because he was about to get some good free food at our expense). All neatly organized thus we entered the marriage venue. It was at once decided that we should immediately go to the dais/stage handover the envelope to the bride, quickly have food and disappear.

However, to our dismay the bride and the groom were not at the dais / stage at that point of time as the marriage rituals had begun. We thus thought we should show our face to sacchu da (as proof that we had come) exchange some pleasantries with him, have our food and scamper. Sacchu was thus located, he was awfully busy though which made our task easier, he seemed happy to see us (though we thought he was calculating how much we would have contributed), urged us to enjoy the food (we did not need this encouragement as we were self-motivated to this end). In turn we spoke highly about the arrangements and how beautiful the couple looked (though we had not seen them yet) and so on and immediately on disengagement from him rushed for the food. The food was lavish, with a good spread and felt sumptuous. Once done we quickly decided to go up to the stage, present the envelope and leave. On reaching the stage we observed that the couple were still not there.

In that moment an idea stuck us. we have had our food which was the objective, the night show movie would begin soon so why not just leave without the contribution. Such a consensus was easily achieved so we barged out of the marriage venue. Once outside each one was returned his contribution amidst joy and laughter, and we happily went to the movie feeling proud of our accomplishment of the day.

The next day in office when we assembled and talked together, we were feeling a bit guilty, had a bit of a discussion around it and finally concluded that Sacchu da could never find out that we had not contributed anything. There were so many people invited and **non-contribution** of five people would hardly be noticed. In any case Sacchu da was on leave for the week.

We all got busy with our work as the week rolled by Sacchu da and the marriage were forgotten and in fact we did not even realize when Sacchu da had joined back. In any case we had a feeling of guilt, so we were probably generally avoiding any face-to-face contact with him too.

However, on fine day Himanshu came around to each one of us in turns and told us to meet him outside the office. Not understanding what the issue was we rushed out of the office to meet Himanshau at a ***Pan Wallah*** across the road.

It was then that Himanshu told us that Sacchu da had called him to thank him and us for attending the marriage. However, Sacchu da with a blunt face had also asked Himanshu that while he was tallying and checking the various gifts and contributions made by various invitees during the marriage he couldn't find any gift or contribution from us which made him wonder whether our contribution/gift had got stolen/lost.

We were speechless and silent and asked Himanshu what he had replied to which Himanshu said that he quietly admitted that we had not made any contribution and without looking at Sacchu Da's face had left from his seat.

Till date we accuse Himanshu of telling the truth. He could have just said that we did contribute, might have got lost. Himanshu however feels that on that day, sitting in front of Sacchu da ***the officer*** the truth was the only thing he could think of......

I dont know whether Sacchu da had another son or daughter. I dont know when they got married. However, I am sure we were not invited...

We had not behaved like An **Officer and A Gentleman** and Sacchu da for sure would have taken serious offence to such **Un-Officer** like behavior on our part.

INERTIA OF MOTION

Genre: Comedy through Physics
Source: Elaboration of a simple Whatsapp Joke

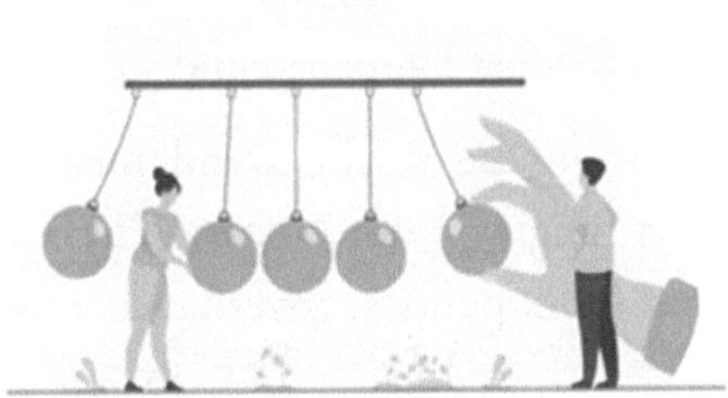

This is a story of physics.

This is also a story of local train commute.

Many will and should relate to it.

Sealdah to Naihati and beyond is a lovely local train ride and I was almost a regular commuter during my days of stay at the town of Kancharapara.

The best option in those days for me of going to Kolkata (Calcutta then) and back was by taking a local train from Kanchrapara and Sealdah and vice versa.

I always enjoyed these train journeys as they opened up a huge canvas in front of me. The multitude and diversity of people in the local trains always lured me.

My favourite position would always be making the journey standing at the door holding the center rod though many times in rush hours this was not possible.

The speeding of a local train and it's slowing down as it approached a station always attracted me. Most of the time if you were a regular you would end up knowing many people and making friends. You would chat with them, play cards with them, gossip, etc, etc.

Even the vendors and hawkers would start getting to know you and if you were absent there would be inquiries the next day as to what happened and so on and so forth.

Every topic in the world found mention in these short journeys ranging from Nuclear Physics to cricket, football, street food, politics, governance, travel.

Stories, gossips, and tales you could revisit and restart the next day from where you left them.

The train journey almost engulfed you with its life and its stories.

If you were a regular commuter, you would also know the various stations enroute, the changing landscape, where there would be maximum rush and where most people would get down, where the train would generally slow down, etc, etc, etc.

It was a Saturday morning when I boarded a local train from Sealdah.

I wanted to go to Jagaddal where I was to meet a friend.

Jagaddal was a relatively new station and not many local trains would stop there. The stations from Sealdah to Jagaddal in a sequence are as under:

Sealdah (Starting Station)

1. **Bidhannagar** *(Earlier called Ultadanga and named after the Chief Minister Dr. Bidhan Chandra Roy. The local train station for going to Salt Lake / Bidhan Nagar)*
2. **Dum Dum** (*The area was home to the Dum Dum Arsenal, a British Royal Artillery armoury, where, in the early 1890s, Captain Neville Bertie-Clay developed a bullet with the jacket cut away at the tip to reveal its soft lead core (hollow-point bullet), known informally as a dum-dum, or more correctly as an expanding bullet. The previous name of Dumdum was "Domdoma").*
3. **Belgharia** *(Once upon a time a big wholesale market for Fish, Jute, and vegetables)*
4. **Agarpara**
5. **Sodhpur** *(A station which always had huge rush and crowd. Also famous for the Khadi Prathistan where historic decisions with regard to freedom struggle were taken by Gandhiji and other great leaders like Subhas Chandra Bose.)*
6. **Kharadha***(The thousands of workers who had migrated here about a century ago from Bihar and Orissa*

form a large part of the populace and give it a distinctive colour)

7. **Titagarh***(Famous for its railway wagon factory)*

8. **Barrackpur** *(The station with a different architecture. Historically, the town was a military and administrative center under British rule and was the scene of several acts of rebellion against Britain during the 19th century. The oldest cantonment in India and the Police Training Academy in West Bengal are both located in Barrackpore.)*

Barrackpore Railway Station

9. **Palta**

10. **Icchapur** *(Famous for the ordanance factory)*

11. **Shyamnagar**

(The name of Shyamngar came from a folk etymology of Samne + Garh which in course of time changed to Shyamnagar. During the rule of Raja Krishnachandra Roy of Krishnanagar, the king gave the village called 'Mulajore' along with a title of RoyGunakar to his court poet Bharatchandra Ray. In memory of Bharat Chandra Roy Gunakar, there is an old and historic library named Bharat Chandra Library. It is situated close to the railway station. Relatives of Rabindranath Tagore had set up Mulajor Kalibari at Shyamnagar)

12. ***Jagaddal*** *(This was where I was headed)*

I boarded a "Kalyani Simanta" Local and gradually as the train moved on many known faces and known passengers started boarding the train at the various stations.

This being a Saturday the crowd was thinner and the "Adda" (A typical Bengali term for discussions and chit-chats held in a group) was better.

It was only during this "Adda" that I was told this train would not stop at Jagaddal and I would have to get down at an earlier or a later station and then move on to my destination on a different train. However, it also came to light that while the train passes the Jagaddal station it slows down considerably (in respect to the people of Jagaddal an informal sort of arrangement till more trains were given halts at this relatively new station) and one could alight from the running train without difficulty at all.

I was skeptical.

While I was a regular commuter and I had seen many people alighting from running trains I had never tried the same myself. I always thought that I neither had the technical know-how to do so nor had the courage to execute such a feat.

Seeing me diffident a large crowd gathered around me to encourage me and tell me that the matter was very simple.

I only had to manage the **"Inertia of Motion Concept"**, alight from the moving train and instead of just landing plumb and halting I just needed to run along with the train for some time.

Ah…… Aha………

This was something I understood having been a physics student. **"Inertia of Motion".**

Inertia is the resistance of any physical object to any change in its state of **motion**. This includes changes to the object's speed, direction, or state of rest. **Inertia** is also defined as the tendency of objects to keep moving in a straight line at a constant velocity.

Some examples of inertia of motion are as follows:

1. A person trying to get down from a running bus falls forward.
2. **The** fruits fall off due to **the inertia of motion** along **the direction** of the wind.
3. **The** swirling of milk in glass continues even after **the** stirring is stopped.

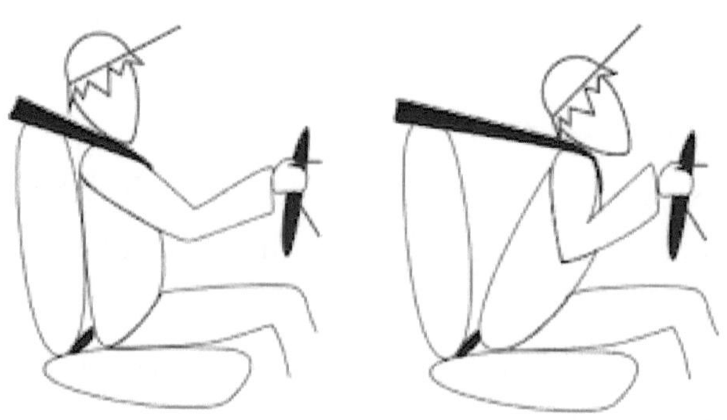

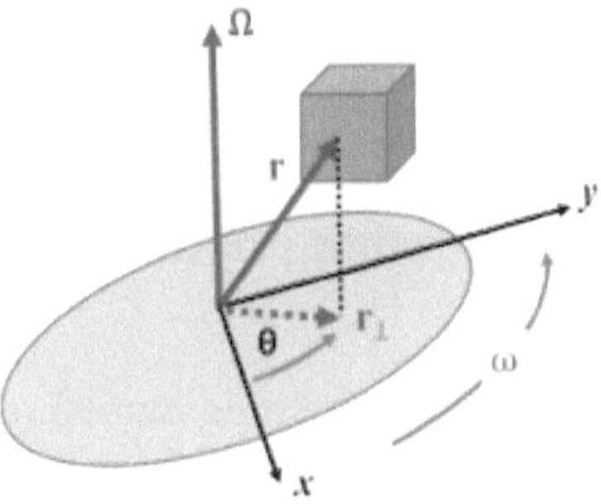

I knew this.

With the concept clear in my mind, thanks to physics, I could nail it.

I thus had to land and keep running so as not to fall. So, my body, when on the train, is moving and if I alighted and just stopped my body would tend to suddenly stop from a situation of motion and I would fall.

I knew this, I had to alight in a running position and keep running for some time to prevent myself from falling down.

Having understood the concept, I had to execute it when the station came, and the train slowed down.

I had good support from the people in the train and numerous examples of people who had pulled it off numerous times even at much higher speeds.

So, when the station came, the train slowed down, and I was ready.

Under cue from a co-passenger, I jumped amidst shouts of **"parbi/parbe/parben"** (You can do it) and kept running.

I half-closed my eyes. I had alighted, I had not fallen, and I should keep running.

I was focused and in a zone. I could hear cheers, claps, and shouts of parben parben, etc. I kept running and running.

Suddenly few hands (helping hands) reached out to me from the train. I was in a daze. In reflex, I grasped one of the hands and felt a few more palms clasping on to me.

I felt a sudden jerk, one of my hands was on the handle of the train at the door, I was running and with a final heave and amidst a lot of claps and cheers I was pulled and hauled up and as I landed and opened my eyes, I was in the train again.

The train was gradually speeding up and the Jagaddal station was passing away and I was on the train.

People were cheering, patting me and saying, "see I said you could do it".

When everything mellowed down, and I had got a seat and could reflect a little I realized what had happened.

Following the laws of physics, I had alighted and started running. The coach from where I had alighted saw me succeed and went back to their own ways.

I kept running keeping the laws of physics in mind and in doing so I had reached the coach ahead and people at that coach thought that I was trying to catch the train.

They cheered me up, few of them reached out and held my hand and with a final heave hauled me in and finally I was back in the same train but in a coach ahead of the coach I was previously in…

I am yet to understand whether studying physics was a good idea at all.

As they say, many a time, **"Ignorance is bliss"**

MISTAKEN IDENTITY

Genre: Humour coarse

Ghosal da pulled a chair in front of me and settled down on it. His big frame made the chair creak ay several of its joints.

He always made the chair creak, and this was no exception.

He had a big and secretive smile on his face.

He suddenly leaned forward, his big belly pushing against my desk, and whispered.

"Minakshi, the name is Minakshi," he said. "The new girl in the procurement department. "Have you seen her?"

I did not look up at Ghosal da and in the same posture told him that I had a lot of work at the office and was really not interested in some girl who had joined some department in our office.

"Shut your work up" whispered Ghosal da a little irritatingly and with displeasure laced in his whisper.

"To become double from single you need to look up and around a bit". he shot back.

Suddenly with an expression of "Oh God" Ghosal da made a mammoth leap from the chair he was sitting on, his belly swiveling and creating waves like a big blob of jelly.

"Come Madam Come, I heard you joined today". I am Sandipan Ghosal, and this is ......"

The newcomer damsel stunned both of us and most of all Ghosal da by saying "I know him, he is PM". How are you PM?"

I felt all the oceans of the world swirling in my stomach, my vision appeared a bit blurred, my mind was blank and just as I was about to pinch myself, I heard the sweet voice again.

"I am sorry, I should not disturb you like this during work". "If it is fine with you, can we not have lunch together?"

"I will drop by to call you at lunch time" "Ok, Take Care".

I shook my head sideways first and then I shook my head up and down with the intention of saying yes while

I watched Ghosal da looking at me with red eyes and I though muttering some of the choicest abuses meant for me albeit with bated breath.

Having settled down on my chair and having come out of the trance a bit I tried to dig into my memory. There was the frock wearing Rimi in our locality, there was Manisha at whom I used to look through the corner of my eye while going to college. I ran my memory thorough my locality, school, college, co commuters, sisters of friends and friends of sisters. I thought of all the girls I had met, tried to scribble their names in my mind, scanned through far and near relatives, even tried a google search but could not recall knowing this beautiful and attractive looking girl even remotely.

My reverie of almost three hours was suddenly shattered by the familiar sweet voice "Come, let's go".

I had been in this office for long 8 years, but this was the first time that I reacted like the rat following the pied piper of Hamlin as I moved towards the canteen.

Enough was enough I decided. It was now time to act smart.

With this thought, some strength returned to me, and I came out with the question in my mind.

"Look do you or rather do I know you". "Am I supposed to know you".

She looked at me directly with her beautiful kohl-lined eyes and said: "you should".

I was now observing her.

She was smiling and I could see that when she smiled a lovely dimple came upon her cheeks. Her eyes were deep and attractive, she had lovely flowing long hairs, she had an elegant taste in terms of her dress sense and her makeup.

"I had heard that you had looked at my photo for a full ten mins and had said No to even considering marriage with me" she had continued while I was observing her.

I had read of a word Flabbergasted in my childhood and today I could feel what it actually meant. I had said no to such a beauty. When? How?

Yes, for matrimonial alliances I have been seeing photos of prospective brides but how did I say no to this damsel.

Minakshi kept talking.

"Amaresh uncle who stays at Topsia is a very good friend of your father". "Is it not". "Had he not gone to your house with the photo of a girl".

I was agape. I could recall a disheveled, darkish photo but… I said Yes.

"That was me" continued Minakshi.

"My parents were after my life for my marriage, but I was not ready. I wanted another year for myself. My mother wanted to send a very nice picture of me, but I had smartly changed it with my Aadhar Card Picture"

I was sitting stunned and bamboozled and staring at the girl of my dreams…

A SHATTERING EXPERIENCE

Genre: Hostel life stunt comedy

The Engineering College hostel had its own distinct identity.

Very often it looked like a ghostly galleon dry-docked in No-Man's Land.

It was displaced and disjointed from the main habitat and populace by a beaten, mud track of almost a Kilometer.

It was a track not oft trodden by most mortals. The forlorn mud track ran parallel to the National Highway 34 bisected by a canal which had no bridges and culverts across the hostel.

On the other side of the mud-track was barren land interspersed with trees, swamps, overgrown bushes and an abundance of stray dogs.

This area thus was a haven for criminals, Illegal activities, and hooch brewing.

The interests of these people were largely mutually exclusive to the interests of the hostellers and therefore the ecosystem ensured peaceful coexistence.

While the mud track was much avoided by civilians and locals the students never had an iota of fear while traversing this path, which they had to do daily to reach the hostel. There never had been any incident where a student had had any misfortune along this track.

At night this track looked like a ghostly ribbon of moonlight with patches of shadows of overgrown trees.

At the end of this track was the main gate of the hostel. A four-storey structure with rooms alongside each other creating in each floor a long corridor from one end to the other. Apart from the staircase and wash-room area, this corridor was lined by a half wall on one side and the rooms on the other side. It was thus like a large balcony stretching from one end to the other. The ends of the corridor in hostel parlance were typically called the wings.

There was such a corridor on each floor with wings at each end.

Each wing in each floor had wooden beds laid out where the "adda" ***(a gathering of people for casual discussions and chit chat)*** would take place. It was here that students sat and smoked, drank, fought, debated and discussed topics ranging from the good-looking daughter of the professor to nuclear science to every other topic under the sun. The wings were thus like the clubhouse of the hostel.

The corridor was, therefore, a place of hectic activity. It was here that the students often played cricket, badminton, football. Many a drunken brawl and fights took place on these corridors. It was here that students also practiced running. Many health freaks also did their exercises on these corridors.

Very often you could see a drunk and tipsy student come out of the room and stutter and stumble along the corridor sometimes alone and sometimes cheered on by other students. At this corridor, many a time would be set up a temporary stage for skits and dramas and the audience would sit along the stairs with their beer bottles, cigarettes, weed etc and enjoy the skit.

The long straight expanse of the wing also allowed abuses and slangs to travel easily from one end to the another propagating the theory of sound waves.

These corridors were also used as dance floors with music blaring from the rooms and students dancing more in mayhem than in rhythm…

These corridors thus had many stories to tell. If only they could speak and yell, if only we could sleep on the corridor with our ears to the floor the corridors and its wings would unfold stories of decades.

This is about one such story.

It was a normal day.

However, there was excitement in the air since morning as a long drinking session was planned in the evening. While alcohol was commonly consumed at the hostel, parties of this type when the entire hostel was involved were few and far in between.

Such events happened when almost 80% of the drinking students agreed to participate and contribute. The teetotalers were in demand on such days as on their square shoulders lay the responsibility of managing a drunk and boisterous gang. Also being students all ran on shoestring budgets and it was a common practice to mix the various varieties of drinks in one or more buckets and the so-called bartender of the day would then serve from these buckets into cups, glasses, earthen vessels, pots and/or any type of drinking container students could lay their hands to.

No money was called for as contribution, but every student was told to bring a bottle of his choice of drink of a particular quantity. The bucket thus carried a medley of brands and liquors creating a huge secular melting pot.

The party started at around 9.00 PM. The bucket with the heady mixture was planted on the bed at the wing. Two bartenders including me were to serve the magic potion and students had already started lining up with their mugs, glasses, pots and containers of various shapes and sizes. The corridor was jam-packed as students collected their drinks and lined up all along the corridor. Once everyone had been served a peg the bell was sounded and was followed by a large chorus of cheers and the party was on its way.

With the progress of the clock deeper into the night the party gradually graduated to the next level when scattered conversations now gave way to a bit of dancing and singing and as the dancing picked up more and more students started joining in. The singing was out of tune and dancing was out of rhythm, but none cared. The non-drinkers were getting busy as steady steps gave way to unsteadiness, the singing became a cacophony and once a while a loud chorus pierced the otherwise silent night. People faltering in their steps were being propped up against walls or were being seated on staircases but often fighting free to claim that they were not drunk.

Time kept ticking and everyone was oblivious to it. The party had crossed the midnight threshold as it was 1 AM. By that time quite a few had to be carried away to their rooms as they were drunk. Some of them who put up the drunken man's fight were taken to the washroom and dunked (this was a common word in the hostel for the therapy which meant pouring a bucket of cold water over a drunken guy to bring him back to his senses) and toweled and sent to their rooms.

As the crowd thinned the group got more closeted.

Antakshri was started. A great game being played by a drunken group added a wonderful twist to the game. Lyrics were either forgotten or made up, rules were forgotten and reminded, the process and sequence were lost and reorganized.

A few more students gradually fell off and went to sleep on the corridor itself.

At around 5 AM with the hint of break of dawn, somebody suggested cricket on the corridor. The idea was immediately lapped up and a group of around 25 still left on the corridor cheered and agreed. Search for a bat proved futile so it was suggested that a T – Square be used as a bat. My room was near to where I was. I rushed in, grabbed my T Square and came out and amidst cheers befitting an opening batsman took to the so-called crease at the end of the corridor. While I stood, took my stance, stared bleary eyes at the bowler's end and winked and winked again to get my vision clear, focused to keep myself steady, the umpire lifted his hands in the air and walked down to me.

Drunken fielders had lined up on either side of the corridor. The umpire called and told me that since a ball could not be found an empty beer bottle was being used as the ball and the umpire felt that it was his duty to inform me. I nodded my head, looked confident and told the umpire to go back and give me a middle stump guard. I was expecting the beer bottle to skid through on the cemented pitch and a middle stump guard would allow me to deflect it on to the leg side.

I saw the bowler running in, the beer bottle glistening in his hand from the first rays of the sun, I opened my eyes wide and focused. The bowler's arms went up in the air and the ball was delivered. I looked at a delivery short of good length, went on the back foot, lifted my bat, heard the sharp swish of something racing across my right cheeks and ears followed by a loud bang and a shattering sound. I felt some fragments hitting me.

I was in a stupor. I remember the students rushing towards me, shaken out of their drunken reverie, lifting me and carrying me to the room and laying me on the bed. They were touching various parts of my body and asking me if I was hurt. I was dazed but felt I was in one piece and said so. Someone shouted he is fine and it's okay and so on.

The beer bottle had skidded across the floor and shattered with a bang against the corridor end wall. Splinters of glass flying off in different directions dawning in the realization as to how foolish and dangerous the idea was. Anyone and most of all me could have been gravely injured.

I heard guys shouting at the guy who had given the idea of using the beer bottle as a ball and the guy defending back saying if his idea was foolish why had the others accepted it. A truce was reached with the realization that all were drunk and high and the mental faculties were not at their best when the decision was made.

Everybody slowly left to their rooms. I moved on the bed into what I thought was a comfortable sleeping position. My head was heavy, and I was feeling dizzy. The drink or the cricket which was to blame I knew not. I folded my hands in prayer to thank the almighty and perhaps succumbed to slumber in that position.

I was taken to the police station and the policemen were all drinking beer from the bottle and laughing at me sarcastically, I was in the courtroom and the judge held out a beer bottle as evidence and asked me if this was the one and before I could reply he said cheers and started drinking, I was in front of the Principal of the college and before I could say anything he had slapped me hard making me wake up with a start.

I looked at my wristwatch beside the pillow. It was 11.30 AM.

I got down from the bed, walked out of the room, into the corridor, which was littered with empty bottles of various kinds, reached the staircase. My eyes were riveted at the Notice Board at the landing of the staircase which said:

NO STUDENT OF THIS HOSTEL IS ALLOWED TO PLAY CRICKET ON THE CORRIDORS WITH BOTTLES OF ANY KIND.

THOSE WHO ARE STILL NOT IN THEIR SENSES AND UNABLE TO UNDERSTAND THIS DIKTAT MAY GET IN TOUCH WITH THOSE WHO ARE.

CART BEFORE THE HORSE

Genre: Office Comedy

When can a horse substitute for a car? That is the question.

What is the thin line of requirement between the horse and the horsepower of a car?

Those who have been fortunate enough to work in a Public Sector Undertaking commonly referred to as PSU would have many stories and anecdotes to narrate.

If all these people could start penning down just one interesting story out of their myriad experiences, it would create copious and interesting literature.

We would have a great compilation of short stories and who knows a very interesting novel too.

This is one from my memory manuscript during my days with a PSU.

Rewind to 1990.

I was posted at Indore, the financial capital of the state of Madhya Pradesh in India, as a greenhorn Officer. Being an engineer, I would have to travel extensively within the state to visit and carry out Risk Inspection of various Industries and factories both in the large and MSME Sector.

The visits to the MSMEs were interesting as they took me to the interiors of the state and often to remote and Godforsaken places to visit small solitary units standing in the middle of nowhere. It was tough too as sometimes I had to stay at run-down motels, pillion ride on someone's two-wheeler on muddy village trucks, eat at roadside dhabas, sometimes even walk miles, but today they make a wonderful memory.

In the process, I visited many interesting places and met many interesting people.

Khargone was one such place and Mr Jain was one such man.

Khargone is a district in Madhya Pradesh and the District Headquarter was in the town of Khargone named after the district.

The district lies in the Nimar region.

In the ancient period, the Haihayas of Mahishmati (present-day Maheshwar: Does that remind us of the Film Bahubali) ruled this region.

Later the area was under the Paramaras of Malwa and Ahirs of Asirgarh. The area was under Malwa Sultanate of Mandu.

In 1531, Gujarat sultan Bahadur Shah brought this area under his control.

Later it passed on to the Mughal Rule as Akbar annexed the territory and later the territory passed through the Peshwas to the Holkars of Indore, Sindhias of Gwalior and Ponwars of Dhar.

Post-independence and merger of the Princely states with Union of India in 1948, this territory became West Nimar district of Madhya Bharat.

Khargone district had been part of the Nerbudda (Narmada) Division of the Central Provinces and Berar, which became the state of Madhya Bharat (later Madhya Pradesh) after India's independence in 1947. On 1 November 1956, this district became part of the newly formed state of Madhya Pradesh.

Jain was a simpleton. He was posted at the Khargone Branch as the Branch Manager. He was thus a Senior Government Officer in a small town and carried this post of his with a badge of honour. In and around he was known as "Manager Sahib" and he quite enjoyed the adulation and the respect and why not as this was quite a big deal for a man from very humble and meagre origins.

He was the Branch Manager of a large PSU, and he was proud of this.

The area at that time was largely a rural area, and his business was confined to insurance of two-wheelers, crops and few cotton ginning and pressing factories. He reported to the Divisional Office at a different location which in turn reported to the Regional Office at the state capital which in turn reported to the Head Office at a

Metro City and for business purposes he often toured the various villages that came under his territory.

One day the Village Panchyat Pradhan told him that being the Manager he should have a car and that would add to his prestige and position.

Mr Jain knew that he was entitled to a car in his current position, and he was also aware of the 80-20 car scheme. As per the car scheme the car would virtually be available to him without any extra cost, and he only had to make an application to the Division Office. The application would then move up the bureaucratic ladder to the Regional Office – Head Office and would return approved via the same route. After that was done Mr Jain could buy the car and start claiming maintenance, fuel and other perks that came with it as per the scheme. Not to mention the pride of owning a car.

Mr Jain decided to act in right earnest. He immediately contacted the Divisional Manager who directed him to

Mr Hamid who was responsible for admin and personnel and handled such matters.

A word or two about Mr Hamid. Mr Hamid was a colorful personality and an interesting character. He believed in living life to the fullest with a smile and he was great at pulling pranks on people without batting an eyelid.

Of course, Mr Jain did not know this.

Mr Hamid placed a call to Mr Jain, introduced himself, in a jiffy made friendship with him and called him over to the Division Office. A date was decided, and the meeting was set up.

On the appointed day Mr Jain reached the Divisional Office with a surreal glow on his face awash with the thought of becoming the proud owner of a car. He was heartily welcomed and greeted by Mr Hamid, and they immediately struck up a chord. In half an hour Mr Hamid knew a lot about Mr Jain, his upbringing, his family, his ambitions, his wishes, his dreams. Very soon Mr Hamid was hosting Mr Jain to lunch at a nice restaurant that boasted of sumptuous vegetarian food.

He was hosting Mr Jain at Company's cost of course.

During lunch, Mr Hamid came to the topic of the car.

"O.P so you want to apply for a car", said Hamid.

"Oh yes", replied Mr Jain.

"Are you aware of the Pros and cons of the scheme and do you realize that in your present posting as Branch Manager of a small town it is not a good idea to go for a car".

Mr Jain was just enjoying the Tomato Onion soup when he was taken aback and looked askance at Hamid.

"Look" Said Hamid, "Car is something you can apply any time you want in your position as Branch Manager, but it does not make sense when you are posted at this branch". "The area you cover is largely rural and most of the villages are better accessed on foot or a two-wheeler and since you have a two-wheeler of your own already you can easily cover these areas on your two-wheeler. Most of the times in the bad roads of the area you would not be able to use the car and the problem will get compounded during the monsoons. The car will mainly lie idle, require maintenance and you would not be able to produce the required fuel bills as you would hardly be able to use it. Since the car would not be used much, you will lose in terms of the maintenance allowances too as these are linked to the kilometer usage of the car".

"You need to think rationally Jain" continued Hamid". "This car would only become a showpiece and would soon become a financial burden on you". "The car is not lost upon you". "As soon as you get transferred to some other place which is urban you can immediately apply for the car". "Only then will the car make sense to you, and I mean financially as well, what with all the allowances and fuel reimbursements and the like". "But Now, not at all".

Mr Jain was bewildered but what Hamid said was making some sense. ""Well Hamid, I get your point, so you are saying I don't buy the car now". "If so what next". This was the Question in Mr Jains mind which he posed to Hamid,

"Aha there you go Jain".

"I knew you were an intelligent dude," said Hamid. "Let us first order the main course"

The menu was decided. Paneer Tikka, Yellow Dal Tadka, Jeera Rice and a Mixed Veg. Items which Mr Jain liked. He was beginning to think that Hamid had something better in store for him.

Hamid was a Pure Non-Vegetarian, and he hated this food, but he knew O.P had taken the bait and that kicked him. In any case Salma, his wife was making Mutton for dinner.

"So, Jain do you know that in such situations the Company has a special provision of providing a horse and only the CMD of the Company has the authority to sanction this".

Mr Jain almost fell off his chair. "A horse" … You mean, "A Horse." He blabbered almost knocking off the glass of water in front of him. With a bewildered expression writ large on his face, he looked up at Hamid.

"That's exactly what I mean", said Hamid with a mysterious smile hanging from his lips.

But Hamid "What will I do with a horse, where will I Keep it, how does it help, I don't know how to ride". Mr Jain was feeling nervous as well as confused.

The Panner Tikka had arrived, and Hamid urged that they start eating.

"Look Jain", continued Hamid. "A horse would mean huge financial gain to you". "The company pays for maintenance and fodder and unlike the car, no bills are required for this as there are no Garages and workshops for horses". "You can thus claim a monthly amount towards these expenses without any bills and this money is yours for keeps". "This is a direct financial gain to you as there is no way one can check and verify these expenses". "And, as for the horse, you can let it graze in the lovely green fields of the village". "The horse grazes for free and you get paid for it". "It's the jackpot Jain". "Very few people know about this scheme, but you are a friend, so I am telling you".

"As far as riding it is concerned you need not ride it". "You can just keep it with you tied outside your house, and we will get one of the village lads to look after the horse at a very nominal cost". "I can reimburse you for this and you can present a handwritten self-declaration towards this expense". "See this bill is in your hands and even if you claim slightly extra no one would question".

"If you so wish you could start learning to ride too". "You could soon be the next Texan on horseback you know".

"Just one word of caution Jain". "Tell no one about this as this is a very special sanction".

"All in all, you thus stand to gain financially to a great extent, and this would not be possible with a car". "The car you can always buy later as per the company scheme". "See you are lucky that you are posted at a small rural place, and you financially stand to gain by applying for a horse".

Hamid sounded genuine and Mr Jain saw reason in what he said, he was starting to get convinced.

The main course had come, and Hamid was enjoying this.

"There you go Jain, "said Hamid. "Now let me tell you how to make an application". "You need to apply on plain paper mentioning your Name, Employee Number, Location, Designation and give brief details of the locality, which I will help you with".

They were into the main course now and Mr Jain was happy with the prospect of getting a horse on Co's money. He had realized that this was a bit of a money-spinner and who did not want money.

The dessert was the only thing that Hamid liked. Jalebis and Rabri.

After the lunch while they walked back to the office, they discussed the process of applying for the horse and that Mr Jain should directly post the envelope to the CMD marking it as Personal and Confidential as this was supposed to be a special sanction resting only with the CMD. Superscribing the envelope as Personal and Confidential would ensure that no one else opened it.

Satisfied thus and thanking Hamid profusely Mr Jain went back to Khargone in the evening. The next few days went into secretive discussions with Hamid and preparing the application. As Hamid had said this was a very special sanction and no one should know about it.

Finally, the application was ready and under the advice of Hamid Mr Jain posted it through the local post office.

He had even calculated the amount of money he could gain monthly in terms of fodder, maintenance of the horse etc.

Almost every day Hamid and Mr Jain would speak to each other and discuss the prospects of the approval of the horse.

In the meantime, Hamid narrated the incident to quite a few people in the Company known to him.

By word of mouth, the news had spread and almost everyone knew that Mr Jain had applied for a horse. Everyone waited for the Head Office to respond. The rumor was circulating but Mr Jain was in a small office in a small town and the news could not penetrate his world of make-believe.

15 days after the posting of this letter to the CMD of Company the landline phone of Mr Malhotra, the Regional Manager rang on a Saturday at 8.00 AM. A lazy weekend when Mr Malhotra enjoyed some extra sleep. He cursed and abused as he awoke dreary eyed from the bed and staggered and stumbled to the phone in his half slumber state, groped for the phone and picked it up.

"Malhotra" the voice at the other end was stern and strong. Malhotra recognized the voice of the CMD (Chairman cum Managing Director) and the slumber left him immediately. He was fully attentive now. "Yes Sir".

"Are we giving horses to our Branch Managers, have you lost it".

Malhotra was dumbstruck but in the next ten minutes, he was given to understand what had happened along with an earful from the CMD inter-alia warning him of posting such foolish people as Branch Managers. In the next half an hour he spoke to his Personnel and Admin Head who knew nothing about it, they contacted the Divisional Manager who knew nothing about it but his gut feeling told him that Hamid might have been involved in this. Hamid was called on his landline and he admitted to this prank.

Both Hamid and Mr Jain were summoned in person to the Regional Office the next working day where they were admonished and hauled up and had to apologise and were let off with a warning.

Later the Regional Manager took Hamid aside and told him not to carry his pranks to a level that the CMD of the Company would get involved and they had a laugh around it.

Over the next few years, Mr Jain had a tough time facing people from the Company as they would laugh both in front of him and behind him. Some would directly ask him about the horse or tell him how foolish and gullible he had been, and he had to carry the embarrassment with himself for long. He was also given various nicknames like Horsey, Colt, Ghoda Babu and so on.

Mr Jain did not speak to Hamid for about a month but finally called him up and vented out hurling abuses at Hamid for making a fool of him. Hamid had expected this and was up for this situation. He charged back saying "Jain, I trusted you, but you let me down and I would not speak to you ever".

"Oh Hello," said Jain "who trusted whom"?

"Jain, I had told you that this had to be a secret as these are special sanctions and I am sure you told somebody and that's why this got messed up". "Come on

Jain" continued Hamid "I tried to help you but ended up apologizing and getting a warning"." This is not done".

Hamid sounded agitated, angry, hurt and Mr Jain again fell for it. He thought and thought.

"Oh Yes Hamid", he said. "I had told this to my friend Pawan the Branch Manager of Datia but I had told him not to tell anyone".

"Now I know," said Hamid "As they say never do a good deed for anyone" and banged the phone down.

Afterwards, Mr Jain made up with Hamid feeling guilty about not keeping a secret but till his last day at the office, he was not sure whether Hamid did play a prank on him.

Had Jain Put his cart before the horse? The readers may decide.

P.S: All names of characters are fictional and any resemblance to any person/place/ thing living or otherwise is purely co-incidental.

IT IS MY KINGDOM, AND I AM THE KING: TRILOGY

Genre: Workplace adventure and comedy

Mr Soni Sigh worked with a reputed Insurance Company in a Division at Delhi.

He was an Assistant Manager and reported to the Senior Divisional Manager.

He aspired to Head a Division one day. The position carried many perks, a nice big office chamber, quite a bit of authority including financial authority, number of subordinates to do the work, a bell to summon the peon, nameplate on the swinging door, a big chair with a nice white towel across the backrest, a stenographer to dictate to and quite a few branch offices with Branch Managers reporting into the Divisional Manager.

There was one hurdle though. The post carried a lot of responsibility and work pressure. This was not something Soni Singh liked. He came from the school of thought "Why take the pressure of work in a public sector".

However, over a period of time, he had realized that if he could head the division in a smaller town he would carry a lot more weight, get more respect and could even throw his weight around.

He would have quite a few Branch Managers running errands for him at his beck and call.

That was not possible in Delhi. Delhi was a big city with 23 Divisional Managers, and he would just be one in the crowd.

He wanted the DM (District Magistrate) feel as Divisional Manager and that was possible only if he headed the Division in a smaller town.

In a year Lady Luck smiled upon him and he was transferred posted as the Divisional Manager of Gwalior.

Encantada- He was enchanted. As the notification and the circular came out the entire Insurance Company came to know about it but hardly did anyone notice the name Soni Singh moving to Gwalior as Divisional Manager heading the Gwalior Division.

Few who knew him congratulated him. While it was a routine office order it was a dream come true for Soni.

He was proven right when three people called him, introduced themselves, welcomed him and said that they were looking forward to his joining. These three were the Branch Managers under the Gwalior Division.

He was over the moon already. He imagined himself like a King sitting on his grand throne.

Soni thus stood vindicated in his own light.

On the appointed day he reached Gwalior to a grand reception by the three Branches and employees of the Gwalior Division. He was garlanded as he alighted from the Shatabdi Express at Gwalior and was whisked away in a car with a motorcade behind him to the Company flat.

A party was hosted in his honor in the evening with the choicest of drinks and lavish food.

He was the hero; he was the king and he braced himself up for a long haul.

Gradually he settled down at Gwalior, came to be known as Manager Saheb, carried quite some powers to his liking and kept on managing the show without taking much of responsibility and hardly ever signing on any paper.

After joining he had made elaborate research regarding his signing authorities and financial authorities and also discovered that more often than not, he could get the officers under him to sign to get the job done.

In certain cases where he had no option but to sign, he had mastered the art of getting sufficient signatures before his signature with adequate justification from them as regards the matter on hand on which the note had been made.

He always remembered the Motto. "Lesser you sign the lesser you would be in trouble".

Let us now explore three incidents considered a master class in the Soni art and art form of avoidance in which he would get famous

The Elusive Chargesheet:

Sharad Kelkar was a Branch Manager under Soni Singh.

He was in his late twenties, recently married and had small material aspirations in life. He had discovered that in order to meet up with these small aspirations he needed a little more money. He found a simple way that of exaggerating conveyance and taxi bills, producing, once a while, fake lunch bills, fake small buys for the branch, like stationery, mineral water bottles and the like. This gave him a bit of extra income and allowed him the material buys he liked like sunglasses, visit fine dine restaurants with his wife, the branded Raymonds blazer. A bit of Peter Scot and such things.

However, he never over did this and kept it within, so to say, reasonable limits.

Unfortunately, as we say smaller thefts have bigger consequences and, in an audit, a snacks bill of INR 100/- got investigated and was found to be fake.

Remember we are talking of 1991 when Hundred Rupees was not as paltry as it is today.

The reimbursement claim was linked to Sharad and an audit recommendation of charge-sheet was put forward. The matter was brought to the notice of Soni as he was the Divisional Manager and as a matter of protocol reported to the Personnel Department of the Head Office of the Insurance Company.

The issued landed upon the table of the then General Manager, Personnel who being an employee-friendly person thought it fit to first speak to Soni Singh about it.

The GM was humane and would generally avoid serious steps unless the matter unequivocally so justified it.

He learnt from Soni Singh that generally Sharad was a decent fellow, ran the branch well and was extremely hard working and dedicated. It was thus settled that the Head Office would only issue a warning letter and call for an explanation from Sharad instead of issuing a charge sheet. As discussed and agreed a warning cum explanation letter was issued and sent across to Soni who was to hand-deliver the same to Sharad and also collect a receipt and a written explanation from him.

It is here that Soni formulated his master plan so as to ensure that Sharad remained loyal to him and indebted to him forever.

He was now in a War Room.

He summoned Sharad to his office, closed the doors to his chamber and in a grave and concerning voice told Sharad that he was in big trouble and a charge sheet, suspension and inquiry was likely. He thus let the sword of Damocles' hanging over Sharad's head.

Sharad was devastated and almost fell to the feet of Soni. The ignominy of suspension would be too much for him and the finding of the inquiry was a forgone conclusion as he knew he had committed this fraud.

Sharad had a family to support and a reputation to protect.

While Sharad cried and wept Soni absorbed and observed him like a dog falling for the bone.

At the final yelp of "Please help me out of this Sir" Soni got up to put his arms around Sharad and told him that he would try his best but, in any case, the charge sheet would be delivered to Sharad and he would first have to reply to the charge sheet following which Soni would try and bail him out.

Thus, partly reassured Sharad left the room and left Soni licking his chops.

Soni Singh knew there was no charge sheet forthcoming. What was coming was only a simple warning letter, but he had ensnared his prey with the intent of making him loyal for life.

One fine morning the Regional Office Dak delivered the warning letter to be issued to Sharad on Soni's desk. Soni opened it, read it, placed it in his upper drawer and locked it. He was now waiting for the prey to wreathe and wriggle.

He decided to hold the letter for quite some time.

After his meeting with Soni Singh, Sharad had been impatient, sleepless and tense and he had been daily calling Soni to find out whether the charge sheet had arrived only to be told Not yet.

This added to his agony.

When Soni finally realized that enough was now enough he eventually beckoned Sharad to his office inter-alia telling him that the charge sheet had arrived.

Such memos always had two copies. One original which was to be delivered and one copy which was to be duly receipted by the receiver under signature to form part of the office file thus creating the evidence that the original letter had been delivered to the intended recipient.

When Sharad arrived Soni Singh again called him inside his chamber which he locked from inside. The atmosphere was still and tense and Soni was looking pensive and anxious too. Soni stealthily opened his drawer and brought out the office copy (not the original). He turned the letter around towards Sharad who was sitting across him and covered the contents of the letter with a file with the lower end of the letter protruding out towards Sharad.

He was like a magician conjuring up a trick and Sharad the audience in total hypnosis.

He told Sharad "Write received and sign it". Sharad had no option. He wrote received, signed the letter and put the date and time. Soni then quickly pulled back the office copy opened his drawer put the letter inside the drawer and locked it again.

Sharad sat there looking at Soni. Soni just looked back and said, "Ok, you can go now". Sharad was clueless and blank. "Sir the original letter Sir, if you could give me so that I can draft a reply". "We shall discuss that later," said Soni. "Now just leave before others get to know about all this". Sharad got up and left.

He called Soni Singh at night asking if he could come over to Soni's house to collect the letter. Soni Singh said, "What's the hurry? You know what you have done you can draft a reply". "But Sir I should see the charges in the letter so that I can reply to aptly Sir, I need your help, Sir".

"Think properly Sharad". said Soni Singh, "and be calm and composed" he retorted and hung the phone.

Soni's beer that night tasted better.

From that night onwards Sharad would daily ask Soni Singh for the original letter and Soni would simply say "Sharad draft your reply, ensure that you have covered all the charges made against you in the letter and stay calm and composed"

It is told that Sharad could never lay his hands on the original letter in spite of trying everything from taking Soni Singh out for dinner, giving him gifts, taking him out for drinks and so on and so forth.

Till the time Soni Singh was transferred Sharad remained his faithful dog and the day he was moving out he quietly told Sharad that he would invite Sharad to his house for dinner when he would give Sharad the original letter.

The dinner invitation never came, and the so-called charge sheet remained undelivered for eternity.

The Water Purifier:

One morning Soni decided to visit his various branches in the city of Gwalior. He thus made a tour to the various branches finally landing up at Sharad's branch.

Sharad went out of his way to welcome Soni Singh (remember he had not yet got the letter). He organized an elaborate high tea in the evening, showed Soni around at the branch giving him high importance and praising him in front of his branch employees.

At the end of the day, Soni Singh told Sharad "Sharad your office needs a nice water purifier". "All of you should have good and purified drinking water. "We should buy one for your office you know" he said.

Like a faithful lapdog Sharad barked, "Yes Sir, I think so Sir". "Let us go and buy it now, "said Soni and the two left for the market the subordinate behind the boss.

They bought a nice water cooler which Sharad paid from office money as it was an official buy. The bill being in Soni's authority he immediately signed it. Sharad then suggested dinner to which Soni readily agreed.

They went to a lovely restaurant and had a lavish drink and meal after which Soni Singh was dropped to his house. Once they reached the porch Soni Singh told Sharad to bring out the water cooler and leave it in his house and Sharad could collect it tomorrow for the branch.

Sharad, always loyal, did as was told.

While Sharad was leaving Soni said goodnight and waved back at Sharad adding "Sharad remember the reply to your charge sheet. I can't buy time for you for ever"

The very next day Soni Singh called the water purifier shop, asked for the mechanic and got the water purifier installed at his own house and Sharad could never ask for it to be given back to the branch office.

Once a while Soni Singh would talk about the importance of purified water to Sharad rubbing salt into his wounds and Sharad always felt that in doing so Soni Singh perhaps enjoyed the taste of the water more.

Why should a Divisional Manager work?

Soni Singh truly believed that at his level he was not supposed to work and was supposed to get work done. More so in a Public Sector job where he was the Ringmaster who only cracked his whip while others worked.

However, his method got into a bit of a hiccup due to a certain situation.

Certain agents started writing letters directly to him over various matters.

Now in a PSU a written letter is a serious thing and Soni Singh felt if a letter was addressed directly to him, he would have to take some actions and decisions which he did not want to.

He thought and thought and come out with a solution. He drafted out a circular to be sent out to all employees and agents working with him and attached to his Divisional Office.

The basic content of the letter was as under:

………………………………………………………

"Everyone is hereby requested to take note that in order to increase the efficiency of the office and to ensure senior management involvement in all crucial matters the following process shall be followed hereon:

1. *Everyone has to maintain strict compliance to work ethics and be responsive to both internal and external customers.*

2. *Each letter received is to be replied promptly and in no case later than 24 hours.*

3. *All letters should be addressed to the Division through me"* …………………………

This created an interesting paradox that if a letter was sent directly to the Division it could not be through Soni and if it was sent directly to Soni then it violated the office circular.

Soni thus created a Catch 22 situation and managed to create affirmation and contradiction at the same time.

P.S: All names of characters are fictional and any resemblance to any person/place/ thing living or otherwise is purely co incidental.

MOUSE THROUGH THE DRAIN

Genre: Workplace humor

The Boss was a scrawny man of medium height.

However, his aura and personality made him tower.

He walked with a distinct and discerning gait, generally spoke with a high pitch, hardly ever smiled without good reason and evoked terror not only amongst his subordinates but also amongst his peers and superiors.

It was felt that keeping distance with this man was a good choice unless circumstances presented you with the Hobson's choice.

To boot, he was a bachelor and having managed to celebrate 55 years of bachelorhood with equanimity and distinction he firmly believed that the institution of marriage was largely meant to produce kids who added to an already teeming population of India and only achieved the dubious objective of bringing the GDP of the country down.

Marriage to him was thus a deprecatory ceremony in the overall scheme of things for the country.

He lived life frugally, travelled to the office mainly by public transport, avoided buying a car which he considered to be more of a liability and ate a very lean lunch at the workplace.

The general rumour was that his dinner consisted of at least three pegs of dark rum with some bread or puffed rice thrown in as accompaniment.

Of his various claims to fame, his demeanor was not one while mannerisms being one, stood out.

He was considered whimsical, moody, of acerbic tongue and off his rockers. He carried all these epithets with ease and stubborn nonchalance.

Despite all this, he did command a lot of respect and admiration for his in-depth knowledge of the subject, his sharp mental faculties and his constant eagerness to keep challenging the vast ocean of knowledge. He was an encyclopedia, a library, and a storehouse of knowledge.

His English speaking and writing skills were exemplary and got him encomiums.

Any officer in front of him was a lame duck and was generally shot down in no uncertain terms for reasons of poor understanding of the subject matter and writing skills. You generally needed to be attired with double bulletproof jackets to enter his cabin and face him but no matter how well you prepared on the subject he would manage to find a flaw, elaborate upon it and prove to you that this was the most basic thing that should have been known to you.

QED.

You thus left his chamber with your head hanging low and your spirits hanging lower into the tide of various eager beavers waiting outside to have a crack at your expense over your fate and count the number of bullet marks on your jacket.

It was another matter that everybody had been riddled with the Bosses' bullets at some time or the other.

During those times the Insurance Companies had standard and conventional products and there were many situations where an existing product could not respond to the requirement. To tide over this situation, most insurance companies issued what was called a "Special Contingency Policy".

The idea of such an Insurance Policy was to provide insurance cover for situations not available under the standard products and not specifically excluded under the standard products. In other words, if there was a novel requirement the requirement would be assessed and analyzed, and a Special Contingency Policy would be issued to cover the situation.

Such policies were custom drafted.

For example, if there was a milk powder manufacturing company which stored its product in warehouses and faced a situation where rodents were damaging and contaminating the product leading to a loss and damage to the product such a situation would get covered by issuance of a special contingency policy.

The authority for accepting and approving such proposals was vested with the Boss at Head Office. The idea was to ensure that such products be discussed and approved at the highest level and not issued indiscriminately and wantonly.

Pran was handling this portfolio then and his call for duty almost daily brought him to the line of fire as he had to analyze such proposals being received from the various offices of the country, prepare a detailed note around them and present them to the Boss for approval, rejection or discussion. The various offices who sent such requests would urge Pran to get the proposal approved by the Boss as the proposal was important to them and would help them make greater inroads into the client and so on and so forth.

Pran had so far been lucky to have survived those years on the battlefield.

Most of the time the Boss would find innumerable technical flaws in those proposals and most of the time rightly so and would thus either shoot them down or call for further details.

His process of filtration was straight forward. If the Company itself could not manage their storage from rodents let not an Insurance Company pay for their mismanagement. He had a good nose for smelling out the real requirements which did qualify for a customized solution through a special contingency policy.

Into this line of fire once walked in Jonathan.

Jonathan was a thorough gentleman and an erudite. He had spent long years at the Head Office and had worked extensively with the Boss. The boss had been largely appreciative of Jonathan's knowledge and style of working and the boss considered him as a nice and bright officer in a crowd of crooks.

There was a bit of uncanny camaraderie between the two.

Eventually, Jonathan was transferred out of the Head office and took charge of a Division as the Divisional Manager. Now, once you become a Divisional Manager your primary focus moves to business development and for the sake of practicality, you learn to sacrifice or bypass certain technical considerations here and there in order to pick up business.

For this very reason, the Boss, therefore, considered most Divisional Managers as useless. For him, they were perfect ambassadors of doom for the Company as most of them hardly understood the subject and those who understood sacrificed most of it on the altar of business development. An action he deeply regretted and spewed venom on the matter whenever he got the opportunity.

One fine day Jonathan referred to me a requirement of a special contingency policy. A large Electric Distribution Company wanted a cover for electric thefts. Therefore, distribution losses through thefts would be quantified in monetary terms and the insurance coverage would pay for such losses.

Jonathan had prepared a detailed proposal right from the stage of electric generation to delivery, excluded normal transmission losses calculated through past averages and even further excluded a certain percentage towards unknown and unexplainable losses. After this, the difference between the generation and the final delivery converted to monetary value would constitute a payable claim under the policy being attributable to transmission theft.

Jonathan was a good soul and while Pran was not entirely convinced about the proposal because of the various technical fall outs that Pran could envisage he decided to give it a shot to try and convince the boss.

Also, Jonathan badly wanted to do this business as he thought this could create a mark for him with the client and give him the much-needed opening to get into their main insurance program which was big and that is where the meat was.

Although Unconvinced about the proposal Pran made a recommendation note and sent it to the boss.

As Pran had anticipated he was summoned by the Boss after a couple of hours and completely taken down due to lack of understanding of the matter.

1. How can such electricity thefts be controlled in India?
2. What was the Corporate themselves doing to curb these thefts?
3. What could be other distribution and transmission losses?
4. How will transmission losses be calculated?
5. How will illegal hooking be controlled?
6. How robust is the metering system?
7. What sort of outage has been factored in?
8. Are there scheduled downtimes?
9. Bla
10. Bla
11. Bla

These were some questions which were thrown at Pran. There were many more and they all seemed relevant.

Pran had no answers.

Pran was told in quite uncertain terms not to play ball with Divisional Managers and with Corporates who in Insurance only tried to find an ally to pass on their crimes and losses without doing much about it themselves.

However, as the Boss knew Jonathan, he asked Pran to call in Jonathan the next day for a discussion.

Jonathan reached Head Office at the appointed time, and Pran ushered him to the boss following him, albeit, sheepishly having once being smitten and with the feeling of at least twice being shy.

After the usual pleasantries, and the boss never spent more than a nanosecond on them the topic was placed on the anvil.

The Boss attacked Jonathan with his volley of questions and soon Jonathan was knocked out flat with no answers and no good reason to do this proposal as it was not making technical and insurance sense.

Jonathan then made a final attempt. He looked at the boss and said: "Boss this business is important as it would allow me a foothold into this big Corporate and this is my chance".

The Boss heard Jonathan out, looked at Jonathan in the eye and without batting an eyelid stood up. I could see his eyes twitching, his hands shaking just a bit, his countenance turning graver, his gaze becoming more piercing and his stance aggressive.

Here was a bull ready for the attack

Pran quickly scampered to the corner of the room.

It was then that the Boss made is now famous dialogue.

"Jonathan you were a bright young lad but now for the sake of business you have forgotten your moorings and your technical knowledge".

"It seems Jonathan with you nowadays there is nothing technical it is all testicle".

He paused and Pran could see Jonathan uncomfortably shifting his gaze.

"Jonathan", the boss continued," you do not have the requisite courage and the ability to enter the corporate through the front door armed with your competence and skill and convince them to give you their main business"

"Instead, you want to enter the house through the drain like a dirty mouse carrying a special contingency policy in your mouth and assuming that you would be invited to the dinner table".

"Grow Up Jonathan and do not waste our time". "The mouse which goes in through the drain generally lands up in the mousetrap".

With that the Boss, without flinching an eyelid walked out of the room banging the door behind us and making sure that the last nail in the coffin was hammered in.

Pran and Jonathan were still in the cabin and from the corner of the room Pran looked at Jonathan and Jonathan looked at Pran and no words were necessary.

NOW YOU SEE ME NOW YOU DON'T

Genre: College life adventure and comedy

The Residential College was an esteemed college.

The college had a strict Zero Tolerance Policy when it came to discipline.

However, there are many Stories of escapades, delinquency, breaking of codes of conduct by students who had just crossed from school life into college life and were in a continuous quest for the elixir of life.

This was a boys' only Residential College.

Boys who had just stepped out of school life into college life with the assumption that college life was fun, provided greater freedom, allowed some sort of a license to indulge in certain activities which were taboo in school and were looking forward to adventure and fun were in for a major surprise.

Within the confines of the hostels of the college, the free spirit of the students blossomed and bloomed, and it was in these hostel rooms, war rooms if you like that many a daring plot were hatched.

Those who have studied there knew but for the benefit of those who have not, it is important to state that the codes of conduct, rules, regulations and discipline at this Institute were stringent and the smallest of breach could lead to the student being expelled from the college and thereby from the hostel.

The expulsion was made out to be a very simple affair almost akin to a surgical strike.

No planning was necessary because the process was simple and defined and the then principal, who went by the nickname ***Paaanchi,*** was an expert in the execution of the process.

The student would be summoned, and **Paaanchi** would just look at him and say **"Baari Chali Ja"**

(Which literally translated meant Go Home).

After the sentence was thus pronounced, a jeep would be sent to the hostel and Paaanchi's warriors would then go to the hostel room of the student thus sentenced, wrap up his bedding, pack his clothes and load them and the student on to the jeep.

The jeep would then drop off the student to his home with a small envelope carrying the expulsion letter signed by the great Paaanchi himself.

Phew, what a farewell...... Lock, Stock and Barrel.

The size and extent of the sin or the breach were irrelevant because for every sin the penalty was capital punishment as described above.

Imagine being expelled for good, mid-year, from a premier institute during your 10 + 2 days.

The one thing, among various other things, that was strictly prohibited was going out of the college and hostel campus without permission. However, this was one often broken rule.

The students followed the simple rule that unless caught you were not the thief.

However, the risk of getting caught and thereafter being expelled from the college always loomed largely.

Talk of the Damocles' Sword. There it was.

There were certain points along the perimeter wall of the campus which were considered safe points for such an escape to adventure and freedom.

These points in the walls were typically called 3.5 (Sade Teen), 4.5 (Sade Chaar) and 7 (Sath).

There were many situations you could get caught.

Found missing from the hostel, found missing from the prayer room, discovered by a teacher/professor outside the campus, seen skeptically and furtively walking towards the wall, worst you could get caught red-handed or red feet, if you may say so, atop the wall perched like the foolish monkey about to eat a stolen banana or about to jump off the wall.

Remember if caught you were debarred.

The jeep, the baadi chali ja…The Lock, Stock and Barrel.

One Sunday morning Rajat had planned a rendezvous with his girlfriend. Rajat had planned to leave the hostel after the morning prayers, scale 3.5, walk down to the main road, take the bus and meet his girlfriend in front of Flury's at Park Street, Calcutta.

After the prayers, Rajat took a bath, changed into what he thought was his best dress – a navy blue trouser and a sky-blue shirt, looked at the mirror, felt satisfied with his appearance and walked down to the 3.5 wall to scale.

No one noticed him and he jumped to the other side of the wall easily. He walked down the small winding road on the other side and reached the main road, crossed the road, and waited for the bus at the bus stop.

This bus stop was two stops behind the bus stop of the college main gate. That is, counting from where he intended to board the bus the college bus stop was the second stop.

He was on cloud nine, he was meeting his girlfriend after long. He got onto the bus with a spring in his step. The bus was reasonably crowded with only one seat vacant, and he managed to grab it. At the next quite a few people boarded the bus and now many people were standing as well as all the seats were taken.

Rajat was humming a tune to himself and thinking of the restaurant he would take his girlfriend for lunch.

The American Choupsey was her favourite.

The bus again screeched to a halt and Rajat looked out. This was the bust stop in front of the college.

Suddenly he saw a flicker of white dhoti and saw a white dhoti and kurta clad person boarding the bus. The all-white dress caught his eye.

Normally the wardens (professors, teachers, hostel wardens) of the college wore all white He peered through the crowd in the bus and his heart skipped a beat.

This was Arun Sir boarding the bus. Arun da was not only the chemistry professor but also the warden of his hostel.

God, if Arun da saw him he would be caught red-handed and expelled.

He shifted slightly uneasily in his seat to hide behind the crowd in the bus and decided to look the other way to hide from view.

After some time, he stealthily looked around from the corner of his eye and discovered Arun da planted not far from him.

His hands holding the roof handle of the bus and he is staring at Rajat. Rajat quickly looked away. He was worried. After some time, he looked back again to see Arun da still looking at him.

Arun da had also inched closer to him. This time Rajat's gaze met Arun Da's and Arun da smiled. Rajat looked blankly at Arun da with a frown and question on his face but did not smile back.

Arun da started pushing the crowd and inching closer towards Rajat and this time Arun da waved at Rajat. Rajat stared blankly again with no- recognition writ large on his face. In fact, he looked sideways to pretend that he was trying to check whom Arun da was waving at.

Arun da was puzzled too and he inched forward gradually till he was standing in front of Rajat. "Rajat where are you going? What are you doing here?" asked Arun da. Rajat looked at Arun da with a puzzled expression on his face. "Rajat I am talking to you," said Arun da touching him on the shoulders as he said so.

Rajat looked up at Arun da with an expression of bewilderment and said: "Are you addressing me". "I am not Rajat". "Hope you are not mistaking me for someone else". Arun da got a bit confused but held his own and said: "Rajat don't act smart". "We will get down at the next stop, we will go back to the college, and we will have a little chat". "Sir", said Rajat "You are mistaking me for someone else and harassing me. I am not Rajat and in any case, I have to get down at the next stop as that is where I live". "Also, what college are you talking about". Having said this Rajat got up and started walking to the front door of the bus.

He walked to the door fast pushing the crowd and yelling "give me room I need to get down at the next stop". He reached the door of the bus and without even once looking back got down at the bus stop leaving Arun da totally bewildered and flabbergasted in the bus.

The place where he got down was the music academy stop of the college around two stops ahead of the main gate of the college. He crossed the road and reached the outer boundary wall, scaled it and dropped himself in.

Now the school, the Music academy, the college were all internally connected. Once inside the campus he started running towards the college. He ran for full 20 mins at full steam till he reached his hostel.

He immediately got into his room changed his dress and wore a dhoti and a kurta, opened his chemistry book, and laid it on the table. He then took his navy-blue trouser and the sky-blue shirt to another hostel room of his batchmate and told him to hide these dresses in his cupboard.

He then returned to his desk in his room and opened the chapter of organic chemistry and started reading or rather started pretending to read.

After about 35 mins there was a sharp knock at the door. Rajat took the book in his hand as if reading and went to the room door and opened it.

Arun da was standing outside.

"Good morning," Arun da said Rajat. "Good morning Rajat how are you" replied Arun da. "I see you are studying "continued Arun da. "Yes, said Rajat, "This chapter of chemistry on Organic compounds is something I have been trying to understand but it is a bit tough for me".

Now Arun da was also the chemistry professor and he said "Rajat can I help you". "Yes, Arun da," said Rajat. Arun da then came into the room and for the next 15 minutes, he explained to Rajat the chapter on Organic chemistry.

When Arun da prepared to leave Rajat walked up to the room door with him thanking him profusely for helping him out with his chemistry lesson.

At the door, Arun da suddenly turned around.

"You know what Rajat," he said and Rajat skipped a beat and stared blankly at Arun da. A million thoughts raced through his mind, he could almost hear the engine of the jeep patiently waiting outside to whisk him away and his heart sank.

"What Arun da," said he as soon he returned to his senses.

"Well, I saw a boy on the bus, and he looked so similar to you that I mistook him for you and tried to talk to him but of course he was taken aback". "I felt you were probably going out without permission, and I wanted to confront you, but the boy was totally confused and said he was not Rajat".

"I then got out of the bus after a few stops and took the return bus and came to your room to check on you and lo and behold you are here in your room studying chemistry".

"What a fool I have been". It's a miracle of God that people who look so alike do exist".

"Yes, Arun da", "Definitely Miracle of God" exclaimed Rajat.

When the summer vacations came Rajat carried his Navy Blue trouser and the Sky-Blue Shirt to his hometown never to bring them again to the hostel.

It is told that his girlfriend had waited for him for 4 hours before giving up (remember there were no mobile phones those days) and they almost broke up till she saw reason when the story was told to her and the batch mate who had preserved the trouser and the shirt swore upon God and provided testimony.

DRONACHARAYA CANNOT LOSE

Genre: Viva-Voce duel and humour

Source: Through a narration by a friend

Sitansu was a brilliant student, rather a genius.

He was the blue-eyed boy of every teacher, gem of the school and both an envy and pride for us friends and classmates.

While most of us would study to clear the exams, he would study to build concepts, something we felt was a foolish thing to do during those days -the 80s of the 20th centuries.

We would often mock him and pull his leg by saying things like he would probably be the next Einstien, Volt or Ampere.

He dismissed these remarks with a cheerful gleam in his eyes and a sweet smile on his lips.

While we tried to be successful, he kept nurturing himself and pushing his boundaries to be capable, the importance of which we all realize now.

We were in the 12th Standard and in those days each subject also carried an internal marking by the college to the extent of 10 marks which got added to the marks you obtained at the board examinations.

Needless to mention these 10 marks were very important. These 10 marks were nuggets of Gold.

This scoring was done through a Viva-Voce by each subject professor.

The college professors were generally generous about it either through liberal marking or through easy questions which allowed students to earn the maximum marks. However, there was one exception, Professor Parimal.

Under his barrage of questions, most would score a 4 or 5 and it was a matter of folklore that even the best minds to have faced the Viva-Voce of this man had not been able to cross the barrier of 8 which stood as a record of sorts for the past 12 years.

To bring forth the essence of this to the fore let me tell all of you that in the other subjects most of the students would generally score a 9 or a 10 upon 10.

With this scenario in front of us, we eagerly waited for the day when our great Sitansu would face the Viva-Voce barrage of Professor Piramal. Let me further mention that this was normally conducted in a hall where a student was questioned by the subject professor individually while all of us could sit and watch and await our turn.

The day arrived, we were all seated in the hall and Professor Parimal was conducting his Viva. At the end of the question-answer session Professor Parimal would generally announce the marks he was giving to the candidate, and we could all mostly hear threes and fours.

Suddenly my name was called out and I walked up to the Professor quite gingerly. I sat on the chair in front of him and he asked me "How much do you think you will score". Well, I was not very confident of myself that too against Professor Parimal so I said, "Sir 2". "Let's see," said the Professor and started his volley of questions. I lasted 10 questions, mostly gave wrong answers at which point of time I could read on the Professor's face that he considered me useless.

He finally stopped and declared a 2.5 and dismissed me. This being higher than my expectations I was fine with it and eager to run away from the clutches of the Professor. So, when it ended, I was very happy and almost ran back to my seat. I generally thought getting a Zero was far better than facing the professor.

While I was scampering back to my seat, I heard the name of Sitansu being called. This was the moment, and I could see all my classmates shifting in their chairs and getting attentive to watch the duel.

Sitansu walked up and sat in front of Professor Piramal.

"So Sitansu you are the brilliant student of the class is it not," said the Professor. "Not really Sir," said Sitansu.

"How much do you expect to score" asked the Professor. "10 Sir said Sitansu".

The Professor almost fell off his chair, looked at us and said: "Boys Sitansu says he will score a 10". Someone among us quipped "Sir he will score a 15 out of 10". "Who said that" thundered the Professor.

We sat there blank-faced and obviously no one owned up.

"So Sitansu" continued the Professor "your friends think highly of you, let us see and for the records let me tell you Sitansu that in the last 12 years nobody has even crossed 8 so let us see how good you are".

With this, the session started.

The Professor started shooting out questions and Sitansu kept answering. After every right answer from Sitansu the Professor would say correct and move on to the next question. After some time, the questions started getting tougher and tougher.

The topic of the questions varied from Light to sound to electricity to dynamics to inertia and so on, but Sitansu kept replying. The session reached a fever pitch and even after 50 questions Sitansu was going strong.

The session was reaching a crescendo and we were all upright and taut in our chairs fully absorbed in this epic duel. You could have heard the pin drop but for the voice of the Professor and Sitansu.

45 Mins and Sitansu was carrying on. The Professor had reached quite a level of physics now which was beyond our comprehension. The questions seemed totally alien to us, but Sitansu kept replying.

The Professor was looking for his first wrong answer which was not forthcoming. The atmosphere was charged. You could almost hear our hear beats. Our eyes were riveted and no one event wanted to blink and miss.

Suddenly we were shaken by the question which came next.

"Tell me about the Ampere's Swimming rule Sitansu" said the Professor. Now that was a very easy question and even, I knew it.

Sitansu too was suddenly taken aback because this question was too easy and a sudden fall from a very high level of questioning. Sitansu looked at Professor Parimal not able to understand the reason for this very simple question. There was a pause in the air as the teacher and the student looked at each other.

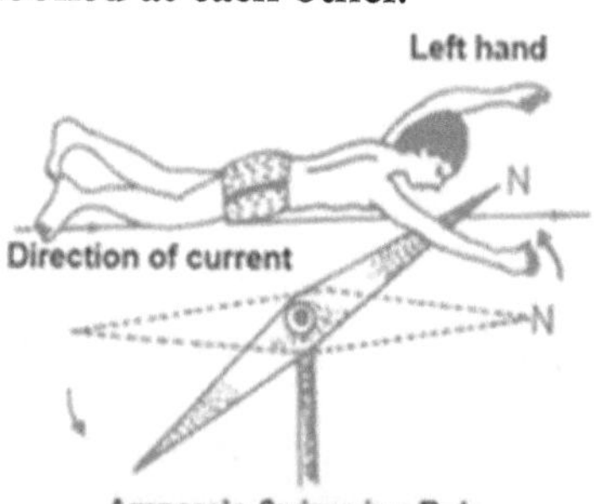

Ampere's Swimming Rule (One can look up this concept of Physics)

Dronacharya and Arjun were locked in visual contact.

For all of us who remember this moment it was a defining moment which lasted for about 40 seconds and is captured in the memory of all of us.

An indelible memory.

"Sitansu, don't you know the Ampere's Swimming rule"?

The Professor's voice pierced through the silence and broke our reverie.

A question is a question is a question and had to be answered. "Yes, Sir," said Sitansu and rattled out the answer.

"Correct," said the Professor.

"Now tell me who taught swimming to Ampere".

That was a stunner and we all almost got up from our chairs too dazed to believe what was happening.

Sitansu looked up at the professor with a bewildered and blank expression. "The answer Sitansu," said the professor.

Now how would Sitansu know who taught swimming to the French Physicist Andre Marie Ampere the founder of Electrodynamics who had also developed the concept of the swimming rule to explain that if a man swims along the wire carrying current such that his face is always towards the magnetic needle with current entering his feet and leaving his head, then the north pole of the magnetic needle is always deflected towards his left hand."

"9.5 and dismissed," said the professor and Sitansu got up to return to his seat. We all spontaneously got up to and started clapping. We saw the professor smiling and clapping too with pride and happiness writ over his face which he was trying to hide.

The perfect ten was not reached technically.

As long as Professor Parimal continued as the Professor of Physics till his retirement the record stood at 9.5 in the name of Sitansu with no one else in all these years even having crossed an 8. We all knew this 9.5 had meant 10 and we are sure Professor Parimal knew that too.

Sitansu and Professor Parimal were in touch as Sitansu ensured that he always remained in touch with the Professor about whom he always spoke highly as someone who made students push the barrier and allowed them to break the glass ceiling.

The Professor had a great admiration for Sitansu and would always talk about him to all his future students.

"I am looking for a Sitansu" he would tell all his future batches.

While respect was mutual how could Dronacharya lose?

P.S:

Dronacharaya:

In the epic Mahabharata, Droṇa (Sanskrit: द्रोण, Droṇa) or Droṇāchārya or Guru Droṇa or Rajaguru Devadroṇa was royal preceptor to the Kauravas and Pandava. He was Arjun's coach.

Arjuna:

One of the five Pandava brothers, who were the heroes of the Indian epic the Mahabharata. Arjuna, son of the god Indra, was famous for his archery (he could shoot with either hand) and for the magical weapons that he won from the God Shiva

SWIM, WRAP & SCOOT

Genre: Engineering college and hostel adventure and prank

This Engineering college hostel was unique. In today's age, it would have been called the USP of the hostel.

Unique Selling Proposition. Huh.

For us, it was a privilege not available to the other hostels or rather not available in most hostels across the country in those times – The 1980s. We not only bragged about it but often misused it as well.

The hostel had a swimming pool attached to it. Let us understand the layout plan a bit as that would be a good reference for understanding and appreciating the incident.

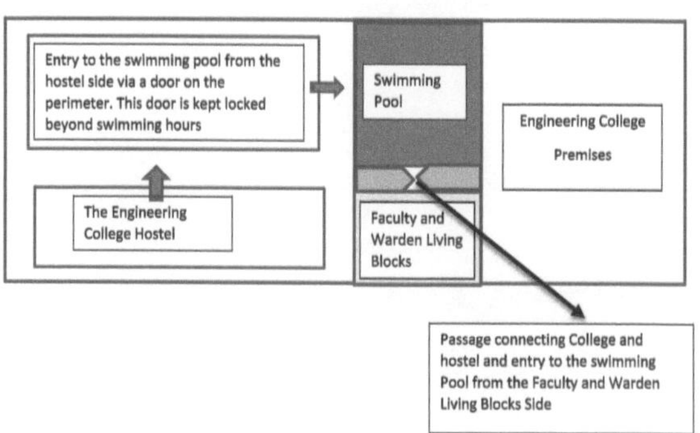

A rough layout of the hostel, Swimming Pool, Faculty Residence and The College

There were strict rules laid out for the usage of the swimming pool and the specified time of use was one of them. These rules had evolved over the years as the swimming pool had been a witness to many incidents like drunk students rampaging the pool, midnight water polo, slips and falls, Daru parties beside the pool, converting the entire pool into a coloured water tank during holi, running in the pool naked and so on.

The knowledge gained through experience of several engineering batches and their pattern of use of the swimming pool had been the genesis for the many stringent rules applicable for use of the swimming pool during our times. Interestingly students kept finding ingenious methods of breaching the rules thereby regularly necessitating updating of the rules.

There were many rules but for the story let us look at a few rules relevant to the story

1. Swimming was allowed from 6.00 AM to 9.00 AM and from 7.00 PM to 9.00 PM only.
2. Drinking was strictly prohibited in and around the pool area.
3. Breach of these rules meant suspension from the college.

This swimming pool was fiercely guarded by the hostel warden Srivastava.

A shortish rotund man known for his penchant for adherence to rules and for his no mercy towards punishment on breach of these rules. He personally ensured that all rules were followed and personally locked both the entrances to the swimming pool from the hostel side and the side of the faculty quarters.

Now in engineering college hostels, the one thing that is obvious and common across the world is the uncanny ability of students to bypass, bend, ingeniously deviate and/or blatantly disregard rules and codes.

This is about once such incident.

It was a lazy Saturday evening, and a party was going on in the hostel room 409 of Jatin on the 4th floor. There was some beer which was flowing and there was singing and dancing. Sometime later in the evening someone mixed some whiskey with the beer and delivered the concoction to everyone. The concoction true to its reputation had the desired effect and the party reached a new philosophical level.

It was around 10.00 PM in the night when someone suggested a swim at the swimming pool. All the eight in the room cheered and with courage stimulated in their inebriated state passed the proposal unanimously and the group of eight sauntered down to the swimming pool a little after having finished their drinks and changed into their shorts and after having picked up a towel each from their respective rooms.

The band of eight in their shorts and towels in hand began their march down the stairs from the 4th floor and towards the swimming pool which looked like the ultimate objective of the night.

The march was quiet and stealthy. Even in their drunken state the students had the sense to tip toe to the pool.

It was around 11.00 PM

Mind you it was outside of usage hours so all the eight had to scale the wall and drop down on the other side. The scaling of the wall was not too difficult, and the stimulation derived from the drinks helped the cause. Once on the other side everyone laid out their towels on the bench, stood up and did a huddle with Jatin clearly stating few rules:

1. No lights to be switched on except the one light inside the pool.
2. No loud conversation.
3. No splashing and making noise.
4. Wrap up in half an hour max.

With this, the party descended into the swimming pool and started swimming. After about ten mins Ajay broke the rule first as he jumped out of the pool, looked at the sky and shouted at the top of his voice "Wow I am loving it".

The seven other bodies in the pool suddenly froze and looked up at him. Ajay having realized his mistake slithered back into the pool and stood inside like a statue. We all looked around trying to fathom how far the sound had travelled. We stood there frozen for about 5 mins observing and trying to gauge any movement at the teachers/warden's block or decipher any light being switched on in any one of the apartments.

After about five minutes we were convinced that nobody had heard us, and we began swimming again. I can tell you the feel of the water with the stars twinkling above you and your mind in the clouds, thanks to the alcohol, is a great feeling.

Gradually the group got a bit fearless and there was some shouting, some jeering, some splashing.

Dutch Courage was clearly taking over.

After some time Jatin called time out and one by one we all scampered up, toweled ourselves dry, removed our shorts which were placed in a small handbag carried by Prakash, wrapped the respective towels around our waist and prepared to leave.

Suddenly like a magician pulling a rabbit out of his hat Prakash pulled out three beer bottles from his bag, brandished them in the air like trophies and suggested a drink. Now in the middle of the night with the cool breeze cutting across this was a difficult to resist proposal and everybody squatted down in a circle on the floor. Prakash said cheers and the group echoed it and the beer bottles were being passed around as we sipped from them one by one oblivious of the fact that the sound waves had now pierced the silence of the night and travelled to the ears of the Warden Srivastava.

Srivastava a man who believed in early to bed and early to rise had gone to bed around 10.00 PM. By 10.15 he was fast asleep and snoring away happily. His slumber was broken at around 11.15 PM. He lay on his bed with eyes wide open.

Did he hear a human sound?

He lay there quietly with alert ears but there was no sound that he could hear. Eventually, after about five mins he dismissed this to some dream and fell asleep again.

Around 11.40 PM Srivastava was awake again. This time he surely had heard a sound. He sat upon his bed and eventually went to the window. It was dark outside, but his ears were alert. He could hear some faint human voices and an intermittent splashing sound. His sensory perceptions could deduce the source of sound to be emanating from the swimming poolside. He was fully awake now. He put on his trousers and t-shirt and decided to check out.

He got out of his apartment and started walking towards the swimming pool. He reached the swimming pool gate, unlocked it and went inside.

He got the shock of his life. Sitting on the floor across the pool where 8 human forms indiscernible and unrecognizable in the very dim light.

Meanwhile, the gang of 8 had heard the clanging of the key against the lock of the swimming pool gate on the other side and were alert.

The gate opened and, in the darkness, they could clearly see the silhouette of Srivastava.

On seeing him they all got up in unison and stood bewildered for about 5 seconds. Then someone suddenly shouted wrap the towel around your face and run. This was like a military command at the war front. We all spontaneously unwrapped our towels from our waist, wrapped it around our face and ran towards the compound wall. It was quite a sight, I guess. 8 naked boys with towels wrapped around their face running towards the wall.

Srivastava was now shouting. "Who is there, stop". We started scaling the wall as Srivastava started zeroing in towards us. Srivastava, as I had said earlier mentioned, was a rotund man and not a fast mover and by the time he could reach close to the wall, the eight naked boys had scaled it and jumped to the other side. His only way to chase them was to go to the gate between the swimming pool and the hostel compound, unlock it and chase the fleeing naked forms.

In the meantime, the eight of us had jumped to the other side and had started running towards the hostel with our towels wrapped around our face and our dinglings hanging out. We reached the stairs and started running up. Sunil suddenly shouted that we all go to Mayanks room on the fourth floor but in the process also run across the length of each floor so that water dripping from our bodies created a confusing trail and did not lead to any specific room.

Finally huffing and panting we all landed up inside Mayanks room and once the lights were switched on for some time the naked truth dawned upon us, and everyone immediately removed their towels from their face and wrapped them around their waist again.

The lights were then quickly switched off and all sat in the room without making the faintest sound.

After about 45 mins nothing happened, and it was clear that Srivastava had given up and gone back to his quarters which was true.

Srivastava on the other hand on opening the gate and having entered the hostel compound was faced with 8 naked bums and backs running into the hostel about 75 meters away from him. He knew he would not be able to catch them and decided to give up the chase and retreat.

Finally, after almost an hour the lights were switched on in Mayanks room and the question in everybody's mind was had Srivastava seen us and could he recognize any of us. Most agreed that since we had our towels wrapped around our face and the light was too dim recognition was unlikely. There was one issue though as Sunil suggested that Srivastava could parade each hosteler naked and try and identify the eight through the manhood of each which he would have definitely seen.

However, this form of identification was considered impractical, and it was impossible to parade around 100 students naked and then try and identify them from the memory of their naked form. Someone suggested that such identification was not legally tenable as well.

Eventually, there was a general strong warning given to the students, few students were pulled aside to check if they knew who these eight were.

Well, in an Engineering College Hostel, there is the "Freedom Fighters Rule" which means no one gives away the names of perpetrators.

The eight of us survived to pass out of the college and carry the incident in our individual and collective memories and there have been many a joke about each other's naked form and till date when there is an argument among any of the eight one of us surely calls out.

"Hey boy, remember I have seen you naked"

DOG CHAIN

Genre: Housing society memorabilia and comedy

Bang Opposite Marwe Gaon (Village), at a stone's throw from the Don Bosco School and within 300 meters of D Mart sprung up a 14 storied residential housing complex – "Testimony Promenade".

The location was good, the railway station was nearby, and the Grand Central Mall was within striking range.

Many apartments in the complex facing the Marwe Gaon had Sea View too. Slightly distant but not too bad. You could see the sea, watch the sun setting on the horizon spreading its golden hue in the simmering water of the sea, seagulls chasing the waves and feel like you are out to the sea.

People looking to buy apartments started purchasing here and the apartments of this 14 storied building started getting sold to various people from various walks of life.

The apartment complex had 60 apartments and an amenities floor which promised a swimming pool, gymnasium, kids' playroom, banquet hall, a gazebo, and a few more amenities.

While bookings would have started much earlier residents started moving in from sometime around January/February 2020.

New owners in their new apartments with obvious glow and pride on their countenance.

The completion work was in progress, but occupancy had begun. For example, the amenities floor was not ready, the backup inverter was not yet upgraded to full capacity, the lift was behaving erratic, the security men and housekeeping staff was temporary, the overhead water tank would tend to overflow and something of this and something of that.

The management of the complex was still with the builder and the "Housing Society" formation had not yet taken place.

Then the lockdown happened and by the end of March, everything came to a standstill. Few families had shifted but many could not.

In the meantime, as the residents got confined to their homes and their residential complexes, they got to know each other, made friends, and eventually formed a Whatsapp Group.

The group started growing and residents started exchanging notes and views in the group. With the partial lifting of lockdown, more families shifted, and people started meeting outside the group too. Social interactions had started growing and maturing.

Gradually the group started feeling the necessity of taking up various pending matters for action with the builder.

To quote a few:

1. Vibrations in the lift and erratic behavior of the lift in the event of power failure.
2. The capacity of the inverter to back up in the event of a power failure.
3. Completion of second-floor amenities.
4. Car parking issues and allotment.
5. Broken and missing floor tiles.
6. Finishing of bathrooms at staircase landings.
7. Fire Fighting equipment usage and demonstration.
8. Managing stray dogs entering the premises and littering the place.

Gradually the group started focusing on issues to be taken up with the builder and champions emerged. Someone knew about inverters, someone knew insurance requirements, someone could analyze the modality and functioning of the CCTVs, and so on.

Through various iterations, back and forth emails to the builder it was finally agreed with the builder that a final list of issues and pending work should be shared with the builder.

The group had started meeting very frequently and as a sequel to various such frequent and in-frequent meetings, a final list of issues/requirements/pending work started getting crystallized.

A final list of 22 issues was posted in the group with the request that if anybody felt that there was any other issue that needed to be added one could do so.

A few people did add few more issues like internet fiber cable line, intercom for the guards at the main gate, thorough and deep cleaning of the drainage systems, etc. However, there was one issue that got posted with a bang and caught everyone's instant attention.

It said, **"Dog Chain"**. This was posted by Hedait Bhai and generated immense curiosity.

It transpired like this (which we all got to know only later) that when everybody in the group saw the post none knew what it meant but everybody thought that the others knew and thus everybody felt embarrassed to ask about it.

Some left it at it as is, some made their interpretation of what it was supposed to mean but the more curious amongst the group called a few others privately to learn more about it.

Prantik was part of the group too and while Prantik had been quite active in listing out issues this one confounded him

The events unfolded as under.

Prantik first called Nihal and found out that Nihal was confused too. In the meantime, Nihal had got quite a few calls as well.

One person had called Nihal to say that he did not need a dog chain as he had no pet dogs and neither did, he intend to own one. However, if a dog chain was given to him, he would be happy to give it to somebody who needed it.

Aha, "A Good Samaritan" at least from the Dog's point of view.

Anand and Sarfaraz who had a technical bent of mind felt that the society would be given few dog chains by the builder which could be kept at the entrance lobby and could be used to chain any stray dogs getting in to be eventually reported to the dog squad of the Municipal Corporation.

They had also started preliminary calculations on the tensile strength of the chain, its length, number of links and had also gone out to identify a place in the parking lot where such dogs could be chained. They were last seen with highly technical and complicated drawings on the various designs of the chain.

Sachin the chief promoter not wanting to get caught with wrong interpretations consulted Saumyadeep and Mukesh and came up with various interpretations of Dog chain the most bizarre being replacing the entire main gate with chains strung from one end to the other.

However, they dismissed this as improbable as they were not able to figure out how residents would maneuver these chains to enter the building complex. The only thing which looked probable was to have residents crawling in from under the gate.

Bhaskaran Sir the matured and technical man in the group with a lot of power plant experience behind him felt that this was perhaps meant to indicate a chain and pulley system for stacking dog houses where pet dogs could reside.

He found this a unique idea and had started contemplating buying a dog as well. This was not the time to bother about the sinusoidal wave form.

Mr. Bhagwat was very busy with a lot of woodwork and interior work going in his house and could not put much thought behind this requirement though the question kept coming back to him and disturbing him like the constant hammering away of the carpenter.

The graceful ladies Shraddha and Shazia thought a chain was not required as they did not believe in chaining dogs. They considered it against animal rights, and they raised a red flag and said, “No Dog Chain is required”.

I am sure the DA (Dogs’ Association) was very happy with this as that day I saw quite a few dogs barking away happily in front of our gate as if to announce look you humans we have friendlies amongst you.

The security guards thought the dogs were openly challenging the residents.

Samant being the quintessential finance man to the core was not worried about what this meant as he had confidence in the idea of Hedait Bhai. He only wanted to check the financial implications of this in the long run.

He had already started working on various spreadsheets. The spreadsheet was almost done except for one formula where he wanted to link the cost calculations to the weight of a dog.

Vikas Kadam and Vijay Babar were slightly confused too but Vikas thought Vijay knew and Vijay thought Vikas knew.

They happened to meet Nihal separately. While Vikas enquired about a cat chain Vijay wanted to know if he could use a leather belt instead of a chain.

Nihal was diplomatic and said that he would confirm with the builder.

One day while rushing to the office Prantik met Sagar at the lift lobby and he said, "Sir get the dog chain done quickly". I said "of course" and rushed off thinking that here was a man who was confident about what it meant.

Prantik admired his intelligence.

While Ranjit said he despised the thought of beating up a dog with a chain Bhavna decided to consult experts in the Middle East who told them that they would prefer to discuss camels rather than dogs.

Prantik was not sure if she will come back with the idea of a Camel Chain.

Das was busy with Mahanagar Gas Connections so he missed the Dog Chain matter and was shaken into conscious cognizance of the matter as various residents started whispering about it. He decided to let dogs lie low and concentrate on the gas connection. Good that he was not deterred by the dog chain else the gas flow into the kitchens of residents would have got further delayed.

Alok Prantik's neighbor, a seasoned shipper, chimed Prantik's doorbell one day. When Prantik opened the door, he found Alok standing with a strange look on his face very much akin to the captain of a ship fearing imminent rough weather.

"I have seen many chains in a ship but not a dog chain," said he.

Well, the inside of a ship was as Greek to Prantik as the surface of the moon, so Prantik diverted the topic by asking Alok whether dogs were allowed in his ship.

Alok said a yes and then a no and then said he would check the shipping Manual for exact rules and regulations on dogs.

Prantik had not heard from him since.

Prantik heard him one day reading aloud ***"The Rhyme of The Ancient Mariner".***

Nihal who by now had become the secretary of the Provisional Committee had to take numerous questions on the dog chain. One day he was found tucked in a corner on the terrace reading a book and making notes.

When asked about what he was reading, he displayed the book. The book was called "Chaining your dog" written by a veterinarian.

Philomina had been busy writing and decided not to bother about the dog chain thereby reposing, sub-consciously, faith in the committee.

Some of the residents thought of consulting Gadekar uncle but normally Gadekar uncle could be engaged only in early mornings during his morning walks on the terrace. Five AM for most was a tough hour to negotiate and engage Gadekar uncle in a dawn discussion on Dog Chains.

The idea was considered inconvenient and dropped.

When the matter had gone round and round and got entangled enough suddenly Saumyadeep posted in the group in Capitals **"WHAT IS THE DOG CHAIN WE ARE TALKING ABOUT".**

The lines descended on the screen of everyone's mobiles, and everyone waited with bated breath for an answer from someone else in the group.

20 mins down and now one had replied. Now it dawned upon everyone that each one was confused. The apple had fallen on Newton's head.

Finally, Sarfraz broke the ***print pause*** and wrote "let us discuss with Hedait Bhai".

Everyone left his/her apartment in their individual capacity to knock at Hedait Bhai's door. While everyone left individually it was a collective gang that eventually landed up at Hedait Bhai's door.

Hedait Bhai opened the door and burst out laughing. He said he had been enjoying the fun for the last five days.

We urged him to explain which he did.

Hedait Bhai had struck upon an idea of preventing stray dogs from entering the premises, so he had thought of chains attached to the lower end of the main gate. He took out a paper and drew and explained. This is what he had meant by "Dog Chain" little realizing then that this would confuse scientists, engineers, accounts, Doctors, businessmen, and everyone else alike.

The students were enlightened, eventually.

The dog chains were finally installed, and this is how they look. Residents have not seen stray dogs inside after that. The committee was then designated to check the working of the chain through a live demo.

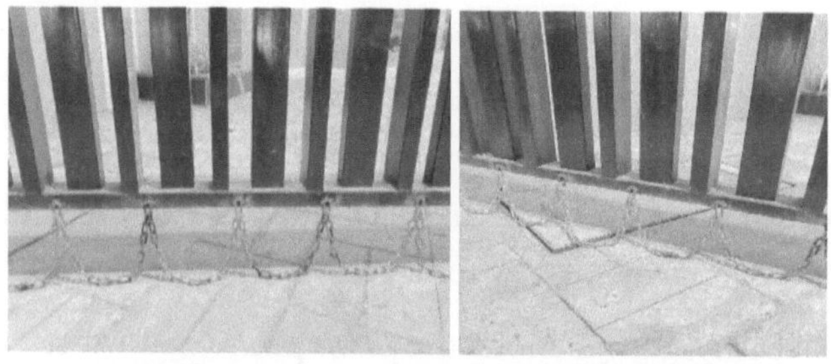

A Close-Up View of the Dog Chains

It was decided to bring five dogs of various sizes and breeds and station them on the other side of the main gate and close the gates. These dogs would then be tempted to try and pass through the main gate by placing dog bones on the other side of the gate and the committee would observe if the dog chain blocked them from crossing over.

The demo was scheduled for the coming Sunday. The committee planned to make it a big event and roped in a celebrity to grace the occasion.

All were invited and urged to get their pet dogs as well.

Eventually Hedait Bhai had the last laugh as the chains held on and dog after dog failed.

Well as they say **"Every dog has his day"**

On Public Demand this event was also streamed live on You Tube.

MOU-CONDITIONS APPLY

Genre: Fictional comedy a tiger and human conversation (A Compilation from a Bengali narrative but changed and further fictionalized)

Banku had fallen asleep. He was deep in slumberland.

The conditions were such. On a steamer, in the lower deck, traveling with tourists through the Sunderban Delta, mangroves all around, the melodious and rhythmic rocking of the boat, the cool breeze, the serenity, the empty bench on the lower deck, enough to stretch legs, lie down and travel to slumberland.

Suddenly a strange smell entered his nostrils. It was a known-unknown smell. He could not recall where he had felt that smell. The steamer was rocking slowly in rhythm to the waves of the delta and the slumber was great.

Where did this smell come from so suddenly?

Banku opened his eyes slowly like a newborn wary of facing the world.

It seemed somebody was lying on the bench opposite. Banku quickly put on his spectacles which he had removed and placed on the bench before falling asleep.

He shuddered at what he saw. Lying on the other bench and staring at him nonchalantly and with utter disdain was a Royal Bengal Tiger. The Panthera Tigris subspecies, native to the Indian subcontinent and the biggest among the wild cats alive today. The National animal of India and Bangladesh.

He could not have out-run the tiger, jumping out of the steamer would have landed him in water and made him vulnerable to more of the species. Therefore, with a pounding and panic-stricken heart Banku just continued to lie on his bench, largely frozen in panic.

Suddenly the Tiger looked at Banku, smiled, and said, "Good Morning".

Without realizing what was happening Banku replied "Good Morning". "It seems you not only can speak but also speak English," said Banku to the tiger in a panic-stricken voice.

"I speak many languages," said the tiger. "I need to" continued the Tiger "since tourists from all over the world visit here it is good to understand their tongue".

"How was your sleep", asked the Tiger.

"Not bad, "said Banku.

"First time in the Sunderbans?" continued the tiger.

Banku nodded in the affirmative.

"Tell me how you would feel if we visited your houses," asked the tiger. "What would you do?" "Would you welcome us in and serve us some fresh deer and allow us to see your house and make friends with your family".

Banku was speechless.

"I know we are not welcome there," said the tiger "why then do you visit our house and disturb us, that too in hundreds and thousands from all over the world". "We are fed up". "Why can't your homo sapiens leave us in peace in our jungle"? The Tiger was visibly angry.

As if a tiger was not enough and Banku now had an angry tiger.

"Well, you see I have not disturbed you," said Banku, "I have stayed put in the steamer and not gone ashore like the other tourists to disturb you and your family".

"Forget it," said the tiger. "Would you like to go to the toilet"?

"No," said Banku. "Why should I go to the toilet"?

"Then I will eat now," said the Tiger.

"What, whom, why?" stammered Banku.

"You of course," said the Tiger.

"Nooooo, why?" Banku shot back in panic.

"Well, we have signed an MOU with the Forest Department you see," said the Tiger licking its chops.

"What do you mean? what MOU, "said Banku gathering some courage to sit upon the bench now.

"We have been promised, as per the MOU, ten tourists per month and in exchange we allow you to visit our jungle and we happily accept your visits without attacking anyone". "As long as the MOU is honored, we behave else we turn man-eaters".

"How does it help you," asked Banku.

"Have you not studied Marketing, are you, not an MBA?" retorted the tiger sarcastically. "Have you not done any projects in consumer behavior, branding, market study and so on and so forth?"

"This will attract more tourists; we will make ourselves more visible and will get spotted easily". "More revenue to the forest department and only then the forest department would be able to honor the MOU of giving us 10 tourists per month". "Simple, attract the consumer and then fleece him". "This is a strategic tie-up."

Banku was under a panic attack now. "But my tour program did not mention this, meaning a tiger can eat me in the steamer itself", replied he.

Banku could now recall the smell. He had got the smell at the Kolkata Zoological Garden when he was standing outside the cage of the Royal Bengal Tiger with his family members.

The tiger was looking amazed now as if trying to assess whether Banku was such a fool.

"You did not read the tour program properly" reverted the tiger with a wry grin.

"What the hell do you mean," said Banku." What was written"?

"Your tour program clearly mentioned in small fonts at the bottom ***"Conditions Apply"*** and it seems like most human beings you did not find this relevant and did not enquire about it". Said the Tiger with an intelligent look on its face. "Had you asked about it they would have told you", added the Tiger.

"You chose me," said Banku crying. "Where is my family," he asked.

"They have gone ashore with the tour guide into the jungle", replied the tiger.

"Will some other tigers eat them too"? asked Banku in tears.

"No", said the tiger, "we follow the MOU". "From one family only one tourist to be eaten is one of the conditions and all tigers strictly abide by this". "We don't look at loopholes in MOUs like you humans do".

Banku realized that he did not have much of a choice. "Will you eat me now or do I have some time", asked he.

"Well, you can take your time". "We have an hour or so in our hands and you can mentally prepare yourself to be eaten and don't try to run because I can easily pounce upon you and catch you and that will make my meal bloodier which can be avoided".

"Should I hold you by the scruff of the neck and take you to the roof of the steamer", questioned the tiger.

"Why the roof"? Banku was unable to comprehend.

"It is nice and sunny on the roof during this winter, and I can enjoy my meal bit by bit on the roof under the sun," said the Tiger.

"You will kill me and eat me and that is enjoyable for you"? "How cruel and stone-hearted are you?". "I have a family", Banku was now desperate.

"I am sure the fishes, birds, sheep, lamb, goat and all the living things that you eat would think the same about you, cruel and heartless". "What do you say to that?" said the Tiger looking angrier than before.

"How is it that I am heartless, sadist, cruel, and what not but you are not". "This is grossly unfair"." I could have moved the courts, but they delay matters". "I cannot wait that long". "In our jungle judgment is quick and fast". "Also, you seem to have preserved your mind in the vinegar of false innocence". "In any case the courts also are run by human beings like you".

This tiger was well-educated thought Banku.

"Come let me take you by the scruff of your neck to the roof". The tiger looked decided.

"I will die", said Banku.

"Only the body dies, don't you know," said the tiger. "Read your Gita". "The soul lives on so do not be so attached to the body".

"Let me now approach you and take you by the scruff of the neck ", said the tiger advancing towards Banku.

Banku is looking at the tiger approaching him. The seat is getting wet, and he can feel it, but he is not able to stop. Suddenly the Tiger's face looks like Pramila his wife.

"Hello Hello wake up "Pramila is yelling at Banku, "you have again wetted the bed, go to the toilet quickly, God I do not know how to manage this". "We will go to the Doctor again today".

Pramila's voice floats in the air as Banku prepares to get up from his bed and go to the toilet. The strange smell continues to linger in his nostrils.

OOPS

HAPPY BIRTHDAY – OOPS

Genre: Ha Ha Ha

Man is a social animal. Who said this? Aristotle of course the legendary Greek Philosopher.

Well, is that Greek to you?

Aristotle did not mention Women, but I am sure he meant to include Women too.

What about LGBQTs? They are social too. Animals are also social. Are they not?

In the Garden of Eden grew the Forbidden Fruit and God commanded that this not be eaten. However, In the biblical narrative, Adam and Eve eat the fruit from the tree of the knowledge of good and evil and are exiled from Eden.

And the Lord God commanded the man, saying, *of every tree of the garden thou mayest freely eat: But of the tree of the knowledge of good and evil, thou shalt not eat of it: for in the day that thou eatest thereof thou shalt surely die.*

The circle of birth-life-death and the procreation evidences the social existence of humanity.

Gatherings Social /Religious / Otherwise, Weddings/ Nikah, Concerts, Sporting Events, Birthday Parties, *Addas* at street corners and *pan walas*. Pubs, Cinema Halls, Rites, and Rituals and even *Janazas* / Funerals indicate how social a human being is. Stick together in life till death do us part and then gather around the mortal body for the last time.

English poet **John Donne**, writing in the 17th century, famously wrote that *"no man is an island,"* comparing people to countries, and arguing for the interconnectedness of all people.

That is enough. Let us lose the philosophy for the time being and cut to the story.

The new normal for social? What is it? "Social Media". Oh Yes.

Facebook, Twitter, Instagram, Tinder, Viber, Hangout, Messenger, Snapchat, Linkedin. Tumbler, You Tube, Bumble, Tiktok, Pintrest, Zoom, Skype, Google Meets, Reddit and **Whatsapp**.

Phew and there are many more.

Millions and Zillions of people connected through all this. Is that Social enough?

This incident is about Whatsapp.

A great feature of Whatsapp is creation of groups for group chats. While some groups are very common like say "1988 Engineering Batch", "Table Tennis Group", "Housing Society Group", "College Project Groups", " Family Groups" and some bizarre groups like " Frusto Group" of frustrated employees, " lunch Munch Group " of office employees having lunch together, " Despo Group ", " *Tharki* Group", " Assholes", fun groups like "Awesome Marathis" of a group of Marathi friends, " Cricket Lovers Group ", "Kitty Party Group" " PNPC Group (*Par Ninda Par Charcha*)etc etc etc.

The list can be endless.

Then there are certain formal office groups. Many a times often created by HR including all employees or a certain level of employees.

In a Company called **Promenade Corporation Limited** a Multinational Company there was such a group called **Team Promenade**.

The group included around 495 and counting employees. This was largely a formal group created by the HR but to some extent was used a bit socially too as people posted jokes, trivia, anecdotes, interesting videos etc apart from HR Communications posted by HR.

Not everyone in this group knew everyone but still most participated even with the unknowns in some form or other.

The popular posts being wishing Happy Birthdays. Someone would know someone's birthday in the group and post "Happy Birthday" and as if like an electric current passing through various conductors everyone in the group would suddenly be jolted awake to wish happy birthday to this person whose birthday it was supposed to be as per the post.

The Birthday Person would then keep posting things like "Thank You", "So Sweet of You", "Thanks for remembering "and so on.

On a typical birthday the birthday messages and thank you messages back from the recipient of the wishes would go on for the entire day depending on who tired out first. While each wished a birthday the poor wish recipient would generally wish a thank you to each and everyone. I am sure by the end of the day the fellahs thumb would be sore enough for cutting a cake necessitating the requirement of a proxy.

It was a bright Sunday morning and Jamlu had just woken up. The first thing he usually did was look at his phone and check for Whatsapp Messages. As he unlocked his phone and went to his Whatsapp a message suddenly popped up in the office group:

"Happy Birthday Sachin", This message came from Huzefa.

Jamlu also quickly typed, "Many Happy Returns of the day Sachin", checked other messages and went about his morning chores. It was 7.00 AM.

He returned to his Whatsapp again at around 9.30 AM. A lot of messages had come in the office group with members of the group wishing happy birthday to Sachin in varying hues, colours and language.

"Takle, Janamdin Mubarak "

"Cake and Thumbs Up emojis and images."

"Where is the party tonight,"? said another.

"How old are you now birthday boy" Someone was curious.

A gif of a glass and drinks bottle where the bottle would jump up and pour the heady concoction into the glass followed with **CHEERS** in bold.

Certain images of Bouquets, Flowers, Cadbury, Burgers, French Fries.

"Where is the cake, Sachin"? said one more.

"How many candles"? said another.

There were certain audio messages too saying Happy Birthday, Birthday Wishes, *Mubarak* and even a Happy Birthday Song.

One employee even got romantic and posted a you tube link to the song "Bachelor Boy "by Cliff Richards. To which some one wrote. "Hey, he is not a bachelor".

This was followed by another link to another song "*Bade Acche lagte hain ......*"

Then someone wrote something in Tamil and someone else almost immediately replied saying "Please Translate".

Taking a cue, the Bengalis Posted something in Bengali and the Marathis Posted something in Marathi and the Kannadigas, Tulus, Biharis, Oriyas, Kashmiris, Assamese all followed suit.

This made Sachin's Birthday very multi-cultural and multilingual. Some understood and some did not, but everybody knew that whatever be the language it was related to the birthday.

After some time perhaps the birthday was forgotten as messages and counter messages became more important and everyone joined the fun thus unfolding. So, people in the group were now chatting with each other triggered by the birthday message of the morning.

Jamlu was thoroughly enjoying this.

However, he suddenly realized that in spite of so many wishes Sachin had not replied at all. There was not a single message from Sachin, not a single Thank you. Now, this was surprising.

"Hey Sachin, where are you", typed Jamlu, "blowing the candles already"?

Everyone else in the group woke up immediately and messages enquiring of Sachin kept popping up.

"Sachin buddy speak up", "*Abe Sachin kuch to bol*", " *lagta hai sala abhi tak so raha hai jaga usko*", " Sir have we got the date wrong"? ""Are there more Sachins in the group?". " *Kal raat ko jyada chada li shayd*".

"Sachin, Knock Knock". Someone tried knocking hard.

"Aree don't worry we won't drop in mate"

The messages were now getting directed to Sachin but still there was no response.

It was around 2.30 PM now.

Suddenly a message from Girija stunned everyone to absolute silence.

"Friends, Sachin is not in this group at all ". Wrote Girija.

There was absolute silence, and nobody wrote for about a couple of hours.

Finally, Pranav wrote *"Bhai Log likhne se pehle dekh toh liya karo ki banda group mein hain bhi ya nahi bus uth ke Happy Birthday likh diya. Kal ko agar Mere Padosi ke bhen ke husband ke bhai ke bacche ke sasur ka janamdin ho to kya is group mein likhoge"*

Ha Ha Ha.

From then Jamlu never wishes anybody Happy Birthday in Whatsapp Groups. He is many a times labelled Un-social for this, but he prefers to be so instead of wishing someone who is not even there to take the wishes.

But after all Man is a Social Animal.

Sorry Women and LGBTQs too.

CORONATION

Genre: COVID times comedy

I am in Business Development. That is the term used nowadays. It just a fancy name for a salesman. Bhai kharid lo chalo powerpoint dekh lo (Brother buy please, have a look at the PPT)

Therefore, I keep hunting for prospects, Murgas (Scapegoats)

In quest of a prospect which was looking very positive, I was to travel to Coimbatore along with my two colleagues. As per regulations, we all had to take the RT PCR as a negative COVID report was required to travel to the state of Tamilnadu.

We gave our swabs on Thursday 24th of March 2021 in the office itself. The phlebotomist poked inside the nose and the mouth with jolly indifference captured and locked the alleged viruses in a small tube and left with the promise of delivering the report by the next day that is the 25th of March 2021.

Our bags were packed, and we were ready to go and since I had to leave from the office itself, I had brought my suitcase in the car to the office after the customary goodbyes, travel safe and come back soon rituals of the family.

The next day I was in an important meeting in the office when one of my colleagues who was to travel with me barged into me and beckoned me to come out of the meeting and follow him. On the way, I was having uncanny thoughts about his gender predilections as he led me to a quiet deserted corner of the office. His expression looked grave and just as I was thinking it was about some business that we might have lost it turned out to be worse. The diagnostic center had called my colleague to inform that I had tested Positive for the ill-famed COVID.

He delivered the news to me, jumped two steps back, and before I could digest it had disappeared from sight.

I was left alone at this quiet corner and as soon as my senses returned, I scampered to my desk, shut down my laptop, and rushed out. I pressed the lift button and scampered in as the lift door opened. Once inside and before the door could shut, I could see Mehul waving at me to hold the lift as he came running to the elevator intending to descend too. I shouted back "No, no"," Positive Positive" and before the elevator door could close, I watched him stop dead on his tracks, turn around and run back into the confines of the office.

I got into my car with myriad thoughts crisscrossing my mind. I had to tell the Driver because my house was about an hour away and I thought the driver should know. I thus sounded him off and to my surprise instead of pulling up at the nearest kerb, opening the door, and running away he stayed put and stepped on the accelerator totally dismissing my condition away.

In the meantime, the news had spread like wildfire in the office, and I started getting calls from various quarters all enquiring about my health and wellbeing. Let it be known that I had no symptoms, but the report was positive and that was what mattered

There was a plethora of advice from different quarters and the various pieces of advice created a strange cocktail. From isolating myself to smelling camphor to bathing with iodine and Dettol to burning neem leaves to inhaling steam to taking Vitamin C and Zinc to exercise.

I called my wife to inform her. She first shrieked in panic and then retorted back with a brilliant idea stating that I should straight go to a hospital or a hotel and quarantine myself more so as my mother aged 77 was staying with us. I suddenly realized that the gravity of the disease was such that I was unwelcome at home though I had no symptoms. I hated John Denver for "Country Roads Take Me Home", well obviously he had sung it in the Non-COVID Era.

Suddenly the driver turned around to ask if I was asymptomatic? I was astounded. Covid had taught quite a bit of medical terminology to everybody. He also asked me if I would have to quarantine myself. I told him that

I had no symptoms and perhaps my Viral Load was less. He told me that all this was a hoax, and I could better check my load through a weighing machine. An increase in weight would indicate virus inside me. I was laughing away at his smart dehati (rural) logic.

However, he stood his ground and advised me not to worry and offered me to isolate myself in his one-room accommodation while he could stay with his friend and take care of me on daily basis.

On the way when my thoughts settled a bit, I called home and told them to prepare the attached bedroom for my isolation all the while trying to sniff and smell various parts of the car on the way to see if there was any loss of smell.

I also decided to rush to the Apollo Hospital near my house to try to do a quick Rapid Antigen Test. Once there I quickly went for a RAT, returned home, and locked myself into the room which was readied for me. I was now in solitary confinement.

The RAT Test report was collected by my driver who called me and immediately started shouting "Sir Negative Sir Negative" as if he had won the Noble Prize.

His happiness was palpable, and I consulted Drs and friends only to realize that the RT PCR was a much more authentic test and for all practical purposes I would be considered positive. That was settled thus, and I braced myself for isolation.

Once inside I felt a sense of relief. I was in a world of my own with my door locked. I had carried essentials inside. An electric heater to allow me to boil water for steaming, betadine liquid, carton of drinking water. A small tool was laid outside my door for the delivery of food and my utensils were segregated.

I thus settled down with my Corona and my Corona combat gear while the rest of the family managed in the other bedroom and the living room.

The first few days were fun. Food would be served to me outside and I would quietly open the door with some warning allowing others to step back a distance, eat quietly, wash the utensils in the bathroom washbasin and keep them outside again. I realized that the food being served to me was slightly special and thought that my condition in the minds of my family warranted special attention to me.

I tele-consulted a doctor who charged me a bomb and issued a long prescription with more of advice and less of medicines. I was told to monitor my temperature and my oxygen saturation every four hours and maintain a chart. I was also told to take vapor at least four times a day.

I would thus pass my days with a set routine. Wake up, boil water on the electric heater, add betadine and inhale vapor, wash my own clothes, clean my utensils, record oxygen levels and temperature every four hours and report to the doctor who generally reverted with a thumbs up and a bill which I had to honor.

My limited knowledge on the subject had told me that the 5th day to the 10th was dangerous. So, as the fifth day approached, I started getting nervous and fidgety. I tried to google my various symptoms only to conclude that I probably had every medical condition in the world except pregnancy.

Inactivity inside the room led to sleeplessness and many times I would wake up in the middle of the night, stare at the ceiling, and finding myself unable to sleep would go about testing myself for symptoms. I was aware that COVID was characterized by loss of taste and smell therefore, many times in the middle of the night I would wake up and go around the bedroom and the attached bathroom smelling things like shampoo, soap, phenyl, colin, harpic, and whatnot.

I was living like a dog with my nose to the ground and smelling away all day.

By the 10th day, I would have given any dog a run for the money in the aspect of smell.

Finding that my smell had not deserted me I would try and check my taste.

However, in an isolated room barred from going outside in the middle of the night what would you try to eat to check your taste. I would thus try and nibble on bars of soap only to spit them out, the taste was intact too without an iota of doubt. I also, after some time started liking the smell of Phenyle and the taste of soap.

After few days I started missing my family members. The pranks and laughter of my daughters the activity of the house, the sight of my wife cooking in the kitchen, the fights, and arguments.

It was all silence with the world happening outside my room.

Many a time I would sit on the balcony watching the activities in and around Karawe Gaon or soak in the sun setting across the creek and watch the bird's fly past.

I particularly made friends with a pigeon who would come daily morning and perch itself on the outdoor unit of my AC and we would talk for hours in some pigeony language. The pigeon taught me perseverance and in my later days of confinement would even refuse to fly away despite me trying to shoo it away.

She was like the dedicated hospital nurse swooping down to check on me every day.

I would also get frequent calls from the Municipal Corporation enquiring about my health only to be surprised to know that I had no symptoms at all. However, their calls never stopped as if they were expecting to see some symptoms develop on me which would probably justify their calls.

Various members of the society enquired about me, and these conversations kept my day going.

Finally, on the 9th day I called for another RTPCR and on the day upon testing negative I emerged from my room and walked into the cheers and smiles of my family members.

I realized how it was without them and I thanked God to have emerged in good health, unlike many others who had not been so lucky.

I silently prayed for those who could not make it out of the ordeal.

My Quarantine was over.

THANK YOU NOTE

Dear Reader,

Thank You for choosing the 'Butterflies in My Bonnet'. It is readers like you who make the effort worthwhile.

I hope you enjoyed the experience of reading the book.

Now, let's take our relationship a step forward by connecting to my social media handles.

Also, if you wish to write personal feedback to me, you can drop me an email at the below-mentioned address. Such personal feedback will help me improve and also give me an opportunity to understand as to where I could improve upon in terms of reader's attention and enjoyment.

I wish you great luck and happiness on your journey ahead full of reading amazing books.

God Bless You!

Instagram – prantikmitra

Twitter - @PRANTIK66

Email - prantik2305@gmail.com

www.ingramcontent.com/pod-product-compliance
Ingram Content Group UK Ltd.
Pitfield, Milton Keynes, MK11 3LW, UK
UKHW040006200726
13854UKWH00001B/63

9 798885 559799